JAKE MARTIN

# SPAWN OF THE BADLANDS

*Complete and Unabridged*

## LINFORD
*Leicester*

First hardcover edition published in
Great Britain in 2003 by
Robert Hale Limited, London

Originally published in paperback as
*Spawn of the Badlands* by V. Joseph Hanson

First Linford Edition
published 2004
by arrangement with
Robert Hale Limited, London

British Library CIP Data

Martin, Jake
   Spawn of the badlands.—Large print ed.—
Linford western library
1. Western stories
2. Large type books
I. Title II. Hanson, Vic J.
823.9′14 [F]

ISBN 1–84395–459–1

Published by
F. A. Thorpe (Publishing)
Anstey, Leicestershire

Set by Words & Graphics Ltd.
Anstey, Leicestershire
Printed and bound in Great Britain by
T. J. International Ltd., Padstow, Cornwall

This book is printed on acid-free paper

# SPAWN OF THE BADLANDS

Butch Keaters, Red McGrath and Slip Anderson were former lawmen who were riding up-country to get jobs on the range. But trouble dogged their trail. Red shot and wounded a crooked gambler and the three men left town with their winnings. Then they were ambushed by three murdering thieves who made them swap horses with them. Now a sheriff's posse identified Butch, Red and Slip as vicious killers. All three were scheduled to stretch rope — but could their brains and gun skills save their lives and bring Colt justice to the killers?

# 1

There were four men at the gaming-table in the corner of the saloon. The one who sat with his back to the wall was a palpable gambler: immobile-featured, stylishly-dressed in broadcloth, his face and his supple hands paler than those of his companions. Sitting opposite him was a younger man also fairly well dressed but with the hard weather-beaten features of one who lived in the saddle, his grey eyes narrow and far-seeing. From under his grey broad-brimmed Stetson flowed luxuriant auburn hair, curling down to the very edge of the gaudy scarf around his neck.

The other two men who made up the quartet were rough-looking nondescripts. Right now they didn't seem to be taking much share in the game. They had thrown in their hands and were watching the duel between the other two.

His face expressionless the gambler shoved another pile of chips to the centre of the table. With a thin smile the young redhead followed suit. As he did so one of the percentage-girls, voluptuous, dark, the pick of the bunch, came up behind his chair and caressed his shoulder. He looked up at her and grinned, his white teeth flashing, a man conscious of his charm over women.

'A mite longer an' I'll be with yuh, Lolita,' he said.

Then his handsome features became set once more as he returned to the game. More occupants of the saloon, which was pretty full, came nearer to watch.

Pretty soon, the only person left at the bar was a huge man in a short plaid blanket-coat, who was wearing, incongruously, on his tough bristly visage a pair of steel-rimmed spectacles. He was tall enough to watch the game over the heads of the others. He didn't seem interested anyway.

Close to him, but on the other side of the bar, a villainous-looking bartender was mechanically polishing glasses.

Perched on top of the bar, at the extreme end, so that he overlooked the gaming-table, was a dark, gangling young man with a vacant expression. He looked suddenly towards the big man. They seemed to exchange glances then the former turned his attention to the game once more. At least he appeared to be looking in that direction — although his eyelids dropped tiredly and his lean body sagged as if at any moment he would topple from his perch.

At the table the two men were watching each other steadily. Lolita was at the redhead's elbow now, her hand at his shoulder, the supple fingers working lightly.

He did not seem conscious of her, he seemed only concerned with his opponent. Suddenly he reached up and caught hold of her hand. She winced as he squeezed it. But his eyes were still on the gambler as he said:

'You're a dirty cheat, pardner.'

The gambler's face did not change expression, only his eyes flamed. His hand slid beneath the table. The Colt that had miraculously appeared in the redhead's fist, boomed deafeningly.

The gambler went back against the wall, which held him up. His face paled, his eyes widened. The derringer he had drawn clattered on the table-top. His hand fell supine beside it. Blood ran between his fingers and trickled along the table-top.

The redhead stood up, his gun still in his one hand, the other clenching Lolita's wrist. The girl squealed as she was swung around the table and propelled to the wall beside the fainting gambler.

'A nice leetle scheme you two have got to fleece the suckers,' the redhead said.

One of the other two men at the table

made an almost imperceptible move-
ment. But the redhead saw it and jerked
his gun threateningly. The man froze.

'This town stinks,' said the redhead.

Across the room the bartender
hauled a shotgun above the bar.

'Hold it, pardner,' a voice drawled.

The bartender lowered the shotgun
cautiously and turned his head. The big
man with spectacles was leaning on the
bar with a Colt held playfully in his
huge hand.

'Slide that blunderbuss along here,
pardner,' said the big man genially.

The barman obeyed with alacrity.
The big man holstered his Colt and
picked up the shotgun. His gaze
travelled along the bar and alighted
on the dark, gangling young man
at the end. The latter still kept his
perch but now he was wide-awake
and upright and had a gun in each
hand.

His voice cut decisively through the
babble around the gaming-table.

'Better let Red thru', you people.

And don't none of yuh get any funny ideas.'

The press parted and Red appeared. Both his guns were holstered now. In his arms he carried a pile of chips.

He planked these down on the bar, saying, 'Cash 'em.'

'You ain't got no right to have all that,' said the bartender truculently. 'You didn't win 'em all.'

'Cash 'em for the gentleman,' drawled the big man at his elbow.

Silently, but quickly and nervously the bar-man spread out the chips and made rapid calculations. Red watched him closely.

Meanwhile the big man regarded all and sundry benignly through his spectacles, the shotgun held steady in the crook of his arm. At their back the crowd were still menaced by the guns of the man on the bar. Nobody moved or spoke.

The bartender shoved a bundle of bills and some coins across the bar. Red collected them up and stowed them in the back pocket of his jeans.

The gangling young man leapt lightly down and joined the other two.

The big man said: 'Everybody stay put. The first one to stick his neck out gets his ears shot off.'

Red had drawn his gun again. The three of them backed to the door.

The three of them went out together. The batwings swung to behind them.

Hooves clattered outside. Bolder members of the crowd moved forward. The shotgun boomed. The batwings swung violently again as a charge of small-shot screamed through them. People became petrified.

Hooves clattered again in the sudden stillness. They were a mere indistinct sound in the night before anybody dared move again.

The shot gambler lay unconscious across the table, his sleeve limp and saturated with blood from the bullet-hole in his upper arm.

Lolita ran outside screaming for a doctor and the law.

7

Butch Keaters removed his spectacles and began to wipe them with a faded bandanna. The sweat boiled from him, making muddy rivulets down his dirty unshaven face. The sun was a brass echoing gong suspended in mid-air.

Red McGrath said: 'Why don't yuh toss them things away. They're nothin' but a darned nuisance to yuh.'

Butch replaced his spectacles and assumed a hurt expression.

'Yuh know I promised ol' Doc Trapps I'd wear 'em.'

'Wal, they make yuh look like a decrepit ol' bullfiddle player.'

'It ain't my spectacles that make me look old,' said Butch gravely, 'it's my grey hairs — brought on by years of watchin' out for you. You an' your fancy women an' your gamblin' an' your temper . . . Why,' he added, 'look at Slip there. Ain't he a wreck? An' all thru' lyin' awake nights worrying over you. Ain't that so, Slip?'

Slip Anderson was slouched in the saddle with his hat pulled over his eyes. He did not look up or give any sign that he was aware of being addressed.

'Hey, Slip!' bawled Butch.

The lean young man started. He jerked erect in the saddle. As if by instinct his hand came to rest on the butt of his gun. He turned wide blue eyes on his companions.

'Yeh?' he said.

They both started talking at once, Red about spectacles, Butch about the other's depredations.

Slip sank his head wearily into his shoulders.

'Ain't no use getting all hot an' bothered arguefying on a day like this,' he mumbled.

Red and Butch looked at each other, shrugged, and grinned. They knew Slip's lackadaisical manner was just a pose; when roused he could be as fast as a cougar. They continued in silence until Red began to whistle a lilting Spanish serenade — doubtless one he picked up in a dance hall sometime while in the arms of a dusky *señorita*. He liked women, but they didn't fool him — as the gambler's sparring-partner, Lolita, had speedily found out.

Butch was wiping his glasses again. He looked at Red. They exchanged disgusted glances.

'I gotta get my hair cut,' said Red.

Butch replaced his glasses and glared at the oblivious and unoffending Slip. Extremes of heat or cold seemed to make no impression on him. He was probably made of whipcord and leather.

The sky above them was a fleckless steel-blue expanse reflecting the vicious rays of the sun. The earth beneath was composed mainly of smooth hard rock which reflected these rays into the faces of the travellers. Only at intervals was it interspersed by patches of sand or lank brown grass and outcrops of rocks like strange growths on its surface. The only vegetation was dead withered trees and clumps of cacti and prickly-pear. The only moving things beside the three humans were the lizards that darted every now and then across their path and, high above, a couple of buzzards hovering, mayhap in anticipation. Before them shimmering like a mirage in the heat-haze were the faint outlines of a row of foothills. They were skirting the border now; its multi-coloured changes of terrain and scenery, its wastes, its ranges, its salt-flats, its lawless territories and its tank-towns. A hard, untamed country.

It was getting on to sundown when they reached the hills. They rested for a while in the shade at the bottom then began to climb the narrow trail.

At the top they reined in their horses and looked back. The sun was going down now and the heat-haze was diminishing. In this short span of time between daylight and twilight visibility was much clearer. The seemingly limitless expanse of the wastelands was spread out below them.

It was Slip who first spotted the moving dots. He pointed them out to his companions. Then he counted them.

'I figure, twenty-two of 'em,' he said.

'Yeh, I got about that,' said Red.

'Shorely it ain't a posse after us,' said Butch. 'If it is they seem to be veering off the track.'

'Anyway,' said the big man. 'I guess we'd better get lower and hole up for a bit.'

They descended the declivity the other side of the hill and broke trail to the right. In a small glade of cotton-woods, a green patch on the slopes, they bedded down the horses. Through a gap in the trees they could see the top of the rise and were within rifle shot of anybody who chanced to appear there.

Twilight fell and they had seen nobody. As the night became deeper and suddenly colder they decided it was safe to light a fire.

'They'd reached here long before now,' said Butch.

'I figured they were takin' another trail,' said Slip.

Red, who was making coffee, said nothing. He opened a can of bacon and beans. He was too darned hungry to talk. Slip didn't seem to need much grub: he'd got no place to put it anyway, and Butch, trying to keep his weight down, was sparing and almost a vegetarian.

Red was the fastest-drawing man of the trio but, squatting on his haunches as he was, he didn't have a chance to do much when the voice called:

'All right, boys, back up. You're covered!'

Another voice snarled: 'Hold it, younker,' and Slip remained poised like a bent bow, his crooked fingers level with his waist.

'Hi'st 'em,' said the snarling voice. 'You, by the fire, get up! Easy now. Hands well up.'

Slowly Red did as he was told. 'Get back with the others,' snarled the voice. Red skirted the fire and joined Slip and Butch.

Three other men came out into the

firelight. The foremost was a carrot-top like Red McGrath only he wasn't so handsome. Far from it. He was thinner, his face pock-marked, his eyes small, glinting evilly in the ruddy glow. He hefted his gun in his hand in a very businesslike manner. His companions did likewise. The big fellow, not so tall as Butch but carrying more in the undercarriage, and the thinnish, darkish nondescript who stalked behind him.

'I'm afraid we'll have to relieve you boys of your horses,' snarled Ginger.

'You'll what?' growled Butch, menacingly.

His opposite number with the protuberance, confronted him. 'You heard what he said.' It was this big fellow's voice the partners had heard the first time. He glared at Butch as if he had taken a sudden dislike to him. He poked his gun forward. Butch shrugged. He couldn't argue with that.

The redheaded snarler speiled again. 'Get 'em, Lafe,' he said.

The darkish nondescript stalked past

the fire towards the partners horses. In doing so he came close to the three men who stood tense with their hands elevated. Red was nearest. He acted swiftly.

He leapt forward tigerishly, low, keeping under the other's gun. Lafe bared snaggle-teeth and swept his arm down even as Red crashed into his knees.

The barrel of the gun crushed Red's hat with a dull crump. Its wearer grunted and fell forward, carrying Lafe down with him.

Butch and Slip both made involuntary movements.

'You're takin' awful chances, boys,' snarled Ginger. The partners stopped in their tracks, watching. Lafe rolled the prostrate form away from him. Then he rose. He lifted his boot.

'Cut it, Lafe,' snarled Ginger. 'Get them hosses.'

Lafe shrugged and did as he was told. He brought the horses back.

'We hate doin' this to you boys,' said

Ginger. 'You're of the same kind as us.'

'Who says we are?' growled Butch truculently. 'Next time we meet, *hombre*, there won't be room for all of us.'

'We need your hosses, pardner,' said Ginger. 'But there's no need for us to part bad friends.'

'Aw, quit the speechifying,' broke in his pot-bellied friend. 'Let's git goin'.'

'Where's yuh brains, Monty?' said Ginger. 'Do yuh want to get shot in the back . . . ?' He addressed Butch and Slip again. 'Jest lift your guns nice an' easy-like, boys, an' toss 'em across here. You first, big feller with the goggles, slowly now, I shouldn't like to hafta kill yuh. Just the one arm. Easy does it.'

With his eyes still fixed balefully on his tormentor Butch pulled out his gun and tossed it across. It landed with a plop. The fat man, Monty, bent and picked it up.

Ginger motioned to Slip. 'Now you do the same. One at a time. Keep the one arm up . . . That's it. Good boy.'

One by one Slip's twin Colts were commandeered by the fat man.

'Now the other gink, Lafe,' said Ginger.

Red groaned as Lafe rolled him over and relieved him of his twin shooters.

'Our guns ain't any use tuh you, are they?' said Slip, who was curiously attached to his own weapons.

'We'll leave 'em back in the brush with our hosses,' said Ginger.

'That's nice of yuh,' sneered Butch. 'You have got hosses then, hey?'

'Yeh, an' you're welcome to 'em. They'll be all right when they're rested.'

'Thanks,' drawled Slip. 'We hope to be able to thank you again next time we meet.'

Ginger bowed ironically. 'Thank you,' he said . . . 'C'mon, boys.'

The three of them mounted. Ginger gave one last ironic wave of his hand before they were swallowed up in the blackness.

Butch and Slip ran to their fallen pardner and sat him up. He opened his eyes. Then he cursed and struggled.

'Where is that skunk?' he said.

'Take it easy, ol' fire-eater,' said Butch. 'You're jest a mite too late.'

## 3

The horse-thieves' own mounts proved to be beasts that had been almost ridden to death. The best of the three, a brown stallion, would definitely not be fit enough to gallop for a day or two.

Butch, who knew all about horses, tended the beasts. His huge hands, which had crushed the life out of more than one man and, curled around a gun, had blasted down many others, could be wonderfully gentle. He had a way with animals. The three ill-used horses responded to him and were bedded down in comparative comfort.

'I guess these three were the ones the posse were chasin',' said Slip. 'They must've been holed up around here some place — probably watched us ride in.'

'They wuz suttinly pressed hard judgin' by the looks o' these pore critters,' said Butch.

Red, who was still nursing a sore egg-shaped bump on the back of his head, merely grunted. He seemed to hold a grudge against his companions for restraining him from lighting out on foot after the horse-thieves.

'I wonder what they done,' said Slip.

'What they done previously is of no interest to me,' said Butch pompously. 'All I know is that they robbed me of my best friend . . . My best friend,' he repeated. 'And for same I intend to make them pay in blood.'

Red gave a loud guffaw. Startled by this sudden show of hilarity from their seething companion the other two turned on him in astonishment.

'It is no laughing matter,' said Butch, but he could not suppress a grin himself.

'Real smart *hombres* we are,' said

Red. 'We suttinly got out-scouted that time. All I want to do is get my hands on that skinny little *hombre* an' I'll die laughing.'

'Wal — we got our guns back anyway,' said Slip, and he patted lovingly the butts of his twin .45s which reposed once more in the holsters fastened to his lean thighs by taut, greased whang-strings.

Just after dawn they left the hills. They travelled slowly, Butch walking beside the brown stallion. He was a good horse and was mending quickly. Doubtless in a few days Butch would have forgotten his old steed and would be calling this one his best friend — which was just his polite way of insulting his human companions.

They were in the grasslands now. Slip's quick eyes picked out a trail; probably that of the three men they sought.

Red cursed hotly. 'If only we could ride,' he said.

They forged on until the hills they

had left behind were only a floating mirage in the heat-haze. The grassland was all around them now, sweeping away to the horizon like a shimmering sea. Not green or blue but a bright yellowy colour which hurt the eyes. It was parched and brittle and the dust rose in faint blueish clouds from beneath the horses' hooves. In parts, where the grass was extra long, the bruised and broken stalks clearly denoted that someone had passed that way not so long before.

The only signs of life they saw were when they came to a sandy clearing and surprised a couple of prairie-dogs squatting outside their burrows. The little animals yelped shrilly and with a whisk of their tails disappeared from sight. For the rest, the inevitable buzzards still lingered, hovering black crosses in the blue immensity above.

'What a country,' groaned Red. 'I'm tired of looking at the angelic countenances of you two galoots. If we wuz to suddenly come upon those three *hombres* I think I'd bury the hatchet and kiss 'em, one by one.'

They did not come upon the three *hombres* but, surprisingly, Red did realize his wish for further human companionship.

As usual, although he seemed asleep in his saddle, Slip was the first one to see the oncoming riders.

'We're bein' invaded,' he said laconically. Ordinarily, they would probably have played safe and let the bunch of strangers eat their dust, but right now, mounted, as Butch put it, on 'three-legged critters' they just had to wait and see how the deck was stacked.

The bunch of riders, about a couple of dozen in all, soon came up to them. They all had their guns out when they surrounded the trio.

One of them, a little tubby man in black, who sat his horse as if he wasn't used to it yelped shrilly:

'That's them all right, sheriff, I can't mistake the red-head and that big feller — he's the one who shot young Jones. I recognize that big brown horse too.'

The sheriff was a heavy, florid-faced man — who wore his star right prominent on the breast of his red shirt. He said:

'Wal, you *hombres* suttinly did a fool trick amblin' across here like this. Walked right into our hands. Where's the money?'

# 2

## 1

Red McGrath was laughing again. He had a peculiar sense of humour. Always after a vicious, murderous outburst of temper he had these fits of inanity.

Butch and Slip didn't see any sense in trying to fight a small army; they surrendered reluctantly to the posse. But it had taken the whole bunch of them to hold down Red, who fought like a couple of wildcats. Only the intervention of the imperious sheriff, who proved no slouch at his job, saved him from being lynched.

Now he was lying on a hard bunk in a very mediocre jail, nursing a fresh crop of bruises and laughing his flaming head off. His two pards, now ensconced in neighbouring cells — the jail had three only — were eyeing him with the astonishment, which even after years of association, the redhead's outbursts never failed to evoke in them.

The fish-faced jailer appeared with a shotgun held ready. At the sight of him Red went into fresh gales of laughter. This custodian, a simple cow-poke named George, who was just earning a few dollars in his spare time, was at a loss. He shook the gun at Red and made little incoherent would-be-threatening noises then, on seeing these were of no avail, turned tail and bolted.

Red subsided at last and said weakly: 'Them three *hombres* suttinly have us hogtied proper. When we rode into this territory it was a huge slice o' luck for them.'

Sheriff Cuthbertson came through. He eyed Red sternly. 'Are you crazy?' he said. 'The jailer tells me you've been laughin' like a jackass.'

'Not me, sheriff,' said Red innocently. 'It's the jailer who's crazy. I said there was something queer about him as soon as I clapped eyes on him.'

'You've got nothin' to laugh at,' said Cuthbertson. 'You'd better tell us where the money is. Maybe it'll go a bit easier for yuh then.'

'What?' interrupted Butch, wrathfully. 'After you reckon we killed a man. I tell yuh we don't know where the money is. We've never seen the money. We've never seen your stinkin' little town before either.'

The sheriff looked pained. 'Shorely you're not gonna keep stickin' tuh that tale are yuh? We know you shot Darkie Blucher the gambler, in the saloon at Jutetown an' we know you came on along here an' stuck up the bank an' killed Jones, the cashier. All we want to know is where you cached the money . . . ' He added: 'I gotta hand it to you fellers for cool nerve. There wuz a posse from Jutetown out after yuh when you robbed the bank here.'

'Like we told yuh before, sheriff, it's all a matter of coincidence an' mistaken identity,' said Butch, as if he was giving a lesson to a child. 'While you're strutting around here pattin' yourself on the back the three men you want, who we've described to you — we've even given yuh the names of two of 'em — are getting away, and the money with them.'

'Mistaken identity!' snorted the sheriff. 'You answer to the descriptions given by people who saw the holdup. An' so do your horses.' He turned directly to Butch. 'You can't fool me with them glasses. I know they're a disguise.'

'I can't see far without 'em anyway,' retorted Butch.

'We told you our horses were stolen an' the bandits left their tired ones in place of 'em,' said Red. 'I admit I shot the gambler at Jutetown. I caught him cheatin'. But we rode right out on to the wastelands after that. We never came near this town.'

Sheriff Cuthbertson shrugged disbelievingly, then put an end to the argument by stalking away.

Slip Anderson raised his head from his bunk and spoke for the first time.

'Waste o' time the whole of it,' he said. 'We gotta quit waggin' our jaws an' begin tuh do some figurin'.'

'Yeh, we're plumb corralled an' no mistake,' said Butch. 'I ain't got no yen to stretch hemp yet awhile.' He removed his spectacles and began to rub them vigorously.

The night, when it came, was moonless. A sly little wind, born in the cold North, whistled across the waist-lands and darted down the streets, two in all, and around the corners of Nivensburgh. Folks shivered and stayed by the fire in their cabins or sought the warmth and gaiety of the Last Chance Saloon. The latter was the most popular place; there was plenty of talking going on there to-night, dark things were afoot. Quite a large chunk of the population were all for storming the jail and stringing-up the varmints who had killed young Pete Jones and taken the town's money. Others said it wasn't right or regular to do things thataway. Cuthbertson was a good man, best leave things to him. He was also a bad man to buck. More people than the three bank-robbers would be likely to get hurt. There was a lot of argufying and drinking and wagering as the night went on.

As the liquor ran more free people began to think a lot about poor young Pete Jones who lay on a table down the street at Cal Jenkin's undertaking parlour. People who had hardly spoken more than a couple of times to the boy in life now began to describe him as if he had been their best friend.

The saloon was overflowing. Quite a lot of humanity spilled out into the street. There was a lot of shouting and even some gun-waving. Then somebody pulled a trigger. Pretty soon Sheriff Cuthbertson and his two deputies appeared on the scene. The sheriff was fairly popular. Some turned round and sided with him. A deadlock was reached and, still arguing, everybody went back into the saloon. The sheriff, who loved to hear the sonorous tones of his own voice, went with them.

Back in the jailhouse the jailer, George, and another deputy, heard the clamour in the street and looked nervously to their guns.

When the din subsided the deputy said: 'The sheriff must've talked them over.'

'Good for him,' said the fish-faced George and relaxing once more in his chair closed his eyes.

But he was not long to be left in peace for, suddenly, from the dark recesses of the cells behind him issued the most gosh-awful catterwauling. It was terrible — like the crying and howling and moaning and groaning of a stricken soul roasting on the hot coals of Hell.

Both George and the deputy sprang to their feet.

'It's that redhead again,' said George wildly. 'He's plumb crazy.'

'He sounds as if he's dyin' to me,'

said the other, as the sounds died down to an agonized moaning. 'You'd better go an' see what's the matter.'

'All right,' said George. He grabbed hold of his shotgun and passed through the door into the cellblock.

The sound, as he had guessed, came from the redhead's cell.

As George entered the passage, Red's companions were both at the bars of their own cells. They looked anxious.

'Hurry, man,' said Butch. 'Do some-thin'.'

'Quickly,' yelled Slip. 'He's liable to die. Pore Red, I figured he wuz sick tho' he never said nothin'.'

Impelled by the urgency of their tones George went nearer. Red was rolling about on the floor of his cell. His eyes rolled. There was white froth at his lips.

As George watched horror-stricken he gave a convulsive kick with both legs and lay still on his back. His eyes closed but still from his lips came low heart-rending moans. White saliva bubbled from his mouth and ran down his chin.

'For Pete's sake do something,' said Butch. 'He may be dyin'. Get him on his bunk, or prop his head up or something.'

Never a very fast thinker, George obeyed orders mechanically. He unlocked the cell-door and trotted inside. He bent over Red and gingerly put his hand behind the fallen man's head. With his other hand he placed the shotgun carefully on the stone floor. Then he reached that hand forward to grasp Red's shoulder. That was the signal for the prostrate form to become imbued with new life.

Steel-like fingers clamped on George's wrists and he was pulled head-first over his patient's body. The same fingers fled then to his throat, strangling his yell. His head was banged twice on the stone floor and he became still.

The deputy ran into the passage, his gun in his hand.

Red confronted him, framed in the open doorway of his cell, the shotgun held waist-high, the muzzle a little elevated, his finger curled round the trigger.

'All right, pardner, start blastin',' he drawled, 'an' I'll blow your head off.'

The deputy gulped and dropped his gun with a clatter.

'C'mon over here,' Red told him. 'Make it snappy!'

The deputy obeyed with alacrity. Red stepped aside to let him into the cell. 'Get them keys an' let my pards out.'

The man retrieved the keys from his unconscious companion's belt and unlocked the doors of the other cells.

Butch bowed ironically. Slip said: 'Where're our guns?'

'In the armoury cupboard.'

'Gimme the key.'

'C'mon back over here, friend,' said Red.

The deputy went back to the cell which housed the unconscious George. As he passed Red the younker swung the shotgun and brought the barrel down on the deputy's head. Without a sound the man went down. Red rolled him away from the doorway and to the side of his pard, the jailer. Then he locked them in.

'You play rough,' said Butch.

'That'll teach these Nivensburgh bozoes not to monkey with us,' said Red. His face was pale now, his grey eyes glittered. He was raring to go. Butch hoped they didn't meet anybody else on their way out — or maybe they'd be blamed for a killing they really did.

They got their guns and passed out through the front door into the darkness of the street. After the comparative warmth of the cells the vicious little Norther bit into their bones. But, due to it, the street was deserted; from the direction of the Last Chance Saloon floated the raucous sounds of drunken singing.

'The stables are round the back someplace,' said Slip.

They skirted the buildings and found the place. The three horses were fed and rested and ready to go. It wasn't till the trio was almost out of town that they were spotted by an old timer who yelled a querulous 'Hey!' Whether he recognized them or not was a moot point. They left him gaping in a cloud of dust.

Red was laughing again. 'What a town!' he said. 'A sleepy hollow full of loons.'

'Save your breath for ridin',' growled Butch. 'If they catch us again they won't be too sleepy or too loony this time to lynch us on the spot.'

## 2

The rest-up in warm stalls had done the three horses a power of good. Now they really got into their stride. To Butch's huge delight his brown stallion led the way. He put this down to his own careful handling of the beast. He certainly could pick his horse-flesh. Unless something unlooked-for happened a posse wasn't likely to catch up with them.

Originally the three partners had planned to ride up country and get a job on the range for the summer. Now they changed their plans, making a detour with the dual purpose of shaking off pursuit and reaching the border where they hoped to get a line on the bank-robbers who were the cause of all this inconvenience. At the same time they hoped to be able to call in at their home town. They might get word of the bandits there, as well as pick up more material help. All three of them had been deputies there, under old Sheriff Kent, until they had the yen to roam.

Dozing in the saddle they rode all through that night. The following morning Slip brought up the van, covering trail cleverly as they broke fresh ones through grassy and rocky country. At noon when the sun was at its zenith, they reached a tract of treacherous salt-flats.

'What a country,' groaned Red.

'This stuff doesn't stretch far,' said

Slip. 'But if we cross it we shall leave our tracks. I vote we make another detour. We should get around along by that bluff there.'

The other two followed the line of his pointing finger. 'Looks like a decent spot to camp,' said Butch. 'I guess we kin afford to now. The horses need a rest.'

'You don't, I suppose,' jeered Red. 'You're the mighty man who can go on forever.'

'Can you?' retorted Butch. 'You look as if you're dyin' in the saddle . . . I cain't say the same for Slip because he allus looks that way.'

'I'll outride either of yuh right now,' said Slip.

Butch said: 'Maybe you could at that.' He removed his spectacles and mopped them. They left white rings where they had been, encircling blood-shot eyes. The rest of the big man's craggy face was almost black by comparison, the stubble on it thick, grimy and bristly.

Red had the beginnings of a flaming beard that showed up startlingly against the muddy colour of his face. His fine riding clothes that had once been so clean and dandy presented now a very dilapidated and dusty appearance. His grey Stetson was blotched with sweat and dirt.

Like Butch said, Slip looked little different than usual, except a little dirtier. And he probably still had more riding in him than the other two.

'All right,' he said, taking the leadership. 'Let's make for that bluff an' find a place to camp.'

The bluff was further than it looked. Halfway, Butch halted his horse and took a swig at his canteen. He pulled a wry face: the stuff had come from a stagnant little water-hole.

'This'll soon want refilling,' he said.

'Should be water somewhere in the country up ahead,' said Slip.

The blazing sun could hardly dry him up any more than he already was. But judging by the perspiration that was cascading from Butch the big man was losing weight at every yard.

'Oh, to be in Texas!' said Red who right now could not find anything to laugh at.

'Won't be long now,' Slip told him.

They reached the bluff, which was comprised of sandstone and sparse vegetation. They lay down on the fine sand in the shade at its base. The horses found shade too and stood listlessly. The men munched sourdough biscuits and took sparingly of the water. Then they stretched out and slept.

It was late afternoon when they set off again. That night they passed over the New Mexican border into the corner of Texas. Not many miles to the right of them was the border of old Mexico.

'Smell that air,' said Red.

'It don't smell no different tuh me,' said Butch. 'An' it'll be just as hot tomorrow.'

'The scenery's better tho'.'

'El Paso's up ahead,' said Slip.

'Yeh, an' I vote we stop off there,' said Butch. 'I could do with a bath, plenty of chow an' some liquor an' a real bed.'

'Yeh,' said Slip. 'I guess we ain't likely to run into trouble in a big town, like El Paso. We might pick up some news about them three *hombres* . . . '

Red was already urging his horse a little faster.

'Quit jawling,' he yelled. 'My tongue's hangin' out.'

## 3

El Paso was a riproaring frontier town. The railroad men were building a line up to it and probably a junction. It was growing all the time. It had a marshal, a bunch of deputy marshals and even a mayor. It had its banker, its doctor, its several undertakers, its storekeepers and its businessmen. The doctor, the undertaker, and the businessmen probably flourished the most. There was only one real 'big business' in El Paso and that was the one of fleecing the suckers and the tenderfeet. Rivalries existed between the various smooth-tongued gents who claimed monopolies on this trade.

For a town of its size El Paso had above its share of saloons, honkey-tonks and gambling-houses. Some of the establishments were all these things rolled into one . . . The stick-up men, the sneak-thieves, the cardsharpers and other riff-raff, male and female flocked to this Mecca from both sides of the border . . . A mere marshal and his bunch of lawmen was of little good in such a turmoil. What was needed was a troop of soldiers.

The marshal was an unscrupulous quick-shooting gent called Max Winters. He valued money and his own skin more than his job. He raked in bounties every now and then from picking up wanted men in his territory. But he was always careful to make sure first of all that the desperadoes had no friends there who might be likely to stick up for them and cause a lot of unnecessary shooting and such-like. With luck, foresight, cunning and the ability to shoot first Max Winters hoped to live to a ripe old age. If a man on the run had influential friends in El Paso, he was soon sitting pretty. Max raked in money this way too. All the businessmen were his personal friends. He was little more than a hired killer hiding behind a lawman's badge. His particular kind of poison was all too common in the West, its only cure was liberal doses of hot lead.

It was nine o'clock of the evening when Red McGrath, Butch Keaters and Slip Anderson rode into El Paso. The night was dark and the Norther whistled down the almost empty street — even Red's beloved Texas was not immune to its depredations. However it had plenty of competition now from the clanking pianos and squealing fiddles and the raucous human voices. The houses of pleasure were packed almost to suffocation and the wind whistled to itself and to whatever stragglers were crazy enough to be outside on such a night.

It shrieked at the three men as they rode slowly down the main street. It was like traversing a tunnel with a giant blowing icy breaths at each end. But they did not make a dash for the warmth and noise of the bright lights as so many before had done: they sought something quieter and they ranged the street until they found it, a frame house with the curt word 'Rooms' inscribed on its fanlight.

The men dismounted and, leaving their horses at the hitching post, mounted the rickety wooden steps.

'No dice unless they got a bath,' said Butch.

They learned from the ancient, bewhiskered custodian in the lobby that there was no baths there but they could have rooms an' get their baths down the street at Gorilla Thomson's place.

'I gotta big room with three beds

that'll jest suit you boys,' cackled the old timer triumphantly.

'Can you rustle us up some grub?' said Butch.

'I can send down the street to Charlie's place for some and git it up to your room.'

'Good for you, oldtimer . . . Wal, first of all we'll go get this bath,' said Butch.

Gorilla Thomson lived up to his name. An exwrestler, he was built like one of the lesser bipeds. His baths were four tin tanks in wooden cubicles. He heated the water in a huge boiler and ran it into the baths by means of rubber pipes. The method was primitive but effective. The place was fairly clean and there was plenty of coarse yellow soap and a scrubbing brush to each man. The partners luxuriated in lather and scrubbed away until the bathwater was like ink. Gorilla's towels were like sacking but they felt like velvet on three glowing newly-born bodies.

'Now for some chow,' said Butch as they left the place. Then he paused in his stride. 'I think I'll go an' see if the horses are all right first.'

When he had made sure that the horses were fed and bedded down to his satisfaction by the pimply youth in the little stables by the rooming-house he went upstairs to his friends.

Pretty soon the same pimply youth, who seemed to be general factotum around there, appeared with their hot suppers and coffee.

'How about getting us something a bit more powerful to kick this down our gullets with?' said Red.

'How about a bottle of red-eye?'

'Shore, pronto.' Red gave him a bill and he scuttled away.

'What a stinkin' life some o' these kids lead,' said Butch. Had he been there to watch the pimply-faced youth as he reached the street he would doubtless have speculated a lot more. The kid went in the opposite direction to the lighted places where it was customary to purchase red-eye.

He halted eventually at a new, square

brick-built building almost at the end of the street. Both its windows were heavily shuttered but, through minute chinks, little specks of light were thrown on the sidewalk. The kid rapped at the door.

'Come in,' said a voice.

The kid opened the door and stepped inside. There were two men sitting in the office. 'What do you want?' growled one of them.

'The marshal. Where is he?'

'He ain't here, Runt, that's sartin-sure,' said the other man with a guffaw.

'It's important. Where is he?'

'Whatever it is, you can tell us,' said the first man. 'We're his deputies ain't we?'

'I oughta tell the marshal,' said the kid hesitantly.

'Wal, he ain't here. We don't know where he is. He might be outa town.'

'Don't horse around, Runt,' said the other one. 'Tell us what you gotta. It ain't a secret between you an' the marshal is it? Whatever it is we'll either

46

act on it or pass it on to him.'

The kid pointed to a Wanted poster on the wall.

'They're here,' he said. 'In Pop's rooming-house. I'm sure it's them.'

'What, the three bank-robbers?'

'Yep.'

'Aw, you're crazy. How do you know it's them?'

'By the looks of them. An' their hosses.'

'Where are they?'

'In the big room at Pop's place.'

'All right Runt,' said one of the deputies airily 'You can go. We'll look into it.'

The youth said: 'The marshal usually . . . ' He paused and stood hesitantly.

One deputy took a coin from his vest pocket and flipped it to him. It tinkled on the boards. The kid bent and grabbed it. Then he scuttled away. As the door closed behind him the two men looked at each other meaningfully.

'They'll keep,' said one of them.

'But how about the marshal?'

'Yeh, what if that Runt . . . ' The speaker did not finish his sentence but rose and began to buckle on his gunbelt. The other followed his example.

# 3

## 1

The plates were scraped clean and the bottle that had once contained potent red-eye was drained and lifeless. Butch Keaters threw off his outer accoutrements and climbed into bed. The springs squeaked agonizingly, then sunk to the shape of his big body.

'You overstepped your diet tonight old timer,' said Red. 'I figure you must now weigh at least a ton.'

'Quit strainin' yourself an' get to bed,' said Butch. 'An' tell Slip there's no need for him tuh go tuh sleep in that chair.'

'I was thinkin',' said Slip. 'Maybe we ought to've scouted around more before we came up here. Those three skunks might be here in town right now.'

'I'd be too tired to do anything about it anyway,' said Butch. 'You jest cain't drive yourself that-away Slip.'

The lean man rose. 'Anyway I think I'll get myself a breath of fresh air.'

'I'd better come with yuh, Slip,' said Red.

'Nope, you stay here. I shan't be long.'

Red shrugged. 'All right.'

As the door closed behind their lean partner the other two men exchanged glances.

'He's got one of his moods on,' said Red. 'Nobody knows what he might get into. Maybe I'd better foller him an' keep an eye on him.'

Butch groaned as he rolled out of bed. 'Wal, you ain't gonna leave me here on my lonesome,' he said. 'Although how I'll manage to crawl about after all I've been through nobody knows.'

'All *you've* bin thru',' snorted Red.

Butch did not notice the sarcasm, he was too busy, with much grunting and groaning and cursing, climbing laboriously back into his trousers. After pulling off this Herculean feat he buckled on his gunbelt.

'Guns!' he said. 'They weigh a feller down . . . But I'd feel lost without mine.'

'You oughta wear two same as me,' said Red. 'Balance yourself better. You're all lopsided now.'

'That's due to that stinking red-eye,' said Butch. 'C'mon.'

Still grumbling he led the way downstairs. They almost bumped into the pimply-faced kid. He gave them a startled glance as he passed.

When they got into the street there was no sign of Slip. He had evidently moved out of the vicinity of the rooming-house to get his breath of fresh air.

'Now what?' growled Butch. 'I've a good mind to go right back to bed an' leave him to it.'

Red knew he wouldn't. He walked down the street towards the bright lights of the honky-tonks. Butch lumbered behind.

Red moved further into the shadows on the board-walk as a party of horsemen rode down the street towards them. They passed, talking animatedly.

Butch drew abreast with his partner. They reached a half-open door from which light spilled on to the sidewalk. From inside came the hum of voices; someone was playing softly on a toneless piano. The window beside the door was heavily-shuttered. Red paused.

'Looks like a gambling house,' he said.

'You go look for Slip in there,' Butch told him. 'I'll go on a mite further. Singly we won't be noticed so much.'

'All right,' said Red. He watched Butch walk away. Then he sidled thru' the half-open door.

He found himself in a long, low smoke-blanketed room. Red knew that to stand long just inside a doorway always invited curious glances. He wended his way among the tables to the small bar at the end of the place — right beside the piano where sat a sleepy-looking Creole who was running his hands lightly over the keys and humming an outlandish melody.

Red's practised eyes ranged the room. At nearly every table games were in progress. Apart from the usual private poker parties and suchlike there were two faro layouts and a roulette wheel. As was usual when he found himself in such a place Red had an urge to buck the tiger. But, for the moment, he stifled it. As he ordered a drink from an unusually affable bartender he was looking around for Slip — although, somehow, he didn't expect to see the lean young waddy there.

He turned to the bartender. 'Quite a place you've got here,' he said. 'An' quite a town.'

'Yuh darn tootin',' ejaculated the man. 'It certainly is a rip-snortin' little burg. Somep'n's happenin' all the time.'

'Never gets borin', hey?' said Red

with a grin. He wanted to pump the man but had to be careful not to awaken suspicion, as direct questioning always did in a town like this. For all he knew, the three men he and his partners sought might be well-known in this haven of lawlessness and have plenty of friends to boot. On the other hand, they might never have been here or, if they had, had passed through unnoticed.

'I guess you get strangers like me passin' through all the time,' said Red. 'You'd hardly notice 'em.'

'Shore thing,' said the barman. 'An' it don't do to ask 'em no questions either.'

'Yeh, I guess so,' said Red. He was disgusted. This guy was friendly but he didn't say a lot. And what he said meant nothing. Still, maybe he stayed healthier that way.

Red figured that if he hung around a bit he might pick something up. The old urge was working again — maybe if he mixed in and had a little flutter . . .

'I guess I'll cut myself in on a game,' he said.

'Best of luck, friend,' grinned the barman.

'Thanks.' Red crossed to the roulette wheel. He didn't want to get deep into a game in case he got held up too long. Roulette was a bit tame but right now it was the best bet. He could leave it when he pleased.

He bought a small stack of chips and laid a third of them on number twelve. It paid off. He began to get interested.

Next time he lost. Then he made a plunge with half of his chips and won again. Nonchalantly he pushed two-thirds of his chips on to number twelve, his first lucky number. The poker-faced croupier watched him narrowly. He knew a born gambler when he saw one. Number twelve came up and Red raked in again. He began to figure it was time he cashed-in. He knew the tables in those places. They were usually rigged. When a player was going too good they were turned against him.

He missed the next turn and gazed nonchalantly around him. Then he stiffened, his eyes narrowing. Across by the door a man was standing looking this way.

Red recognized him immediately. It was one of the men he sought. It was the dark snaggled-toothed runt who had slugged him.

The runt recognized him too. He turned and went outside.

Red quitted the table suddenly, leaving his chips to spill over on to the floor.

'Hey,' said the croupier. But the redhead was already yards away, causing outspoken comments as he brushed people unceremoniously aside. Next moment he reached the door.

Red's hand was on his gun as he stepped quickly outside. He flattened himself against the wall beside the door. He paused a moment to let his eyes get accustomed to the sudden darkness.

He looked quickly up and down the street. He had a quick glimpse of a dark figure whisking around the corner. He wasn't sure whether it was his quarry or not but he decided to take a chance.

Keeping in the shadows he followed. A bunch of men came out of a lighted place across the street. Red walked smartly like a man in a hurry, his arms swinging. He didn't want to arouse suspicion. But it was doubtful whether the men, who were having a noisy altercation, even noticed him.

Red reached the corner he sought. He looked all around him quickly, then slid around it, his hand on his gun. He found himself in an alley. It was black, silent except for the keen wind whistling down it.

Red went slowly, brushing the wall, his gun out now, his eyes striving to pierce the blackness. He reached the other end and here, although the night was dark, vision was much clearer.

He found himself in one of the small backwaters of the town, a short cul-de-sac of small log, frame and adobe cabins. It was then he saw the figure again, at the end of the street. As he watched, it vanished. Whether the man had seen him or not he did not know. And still he was not sure whether it was the man he sought. Again he had to take a chance.

Luckily the street was sod beneath his feet instead of hard rock or pebbles. There were no sidewalks. Some of the cabins had stoops, small verandas or porches before their doors, others opened directly on the street. Red walked at a nice easy pace past them, past the lighted windows and the dark ones that seemed doubly dangerous, from behind whose seemingly-sightless façades, eyes might watch, guns be levelled. Again Red gave the impression of a man with an errand, but without that added urgency that might cause comment. All the time he was keyed up like a bunch of steel springs, ready to fall flat or leap aside, gun drawn and spitting lead. He saw no one. He heard nothing.

He was approaching the point where

the man had disappeared. The next building was a squat adobe dwelling. Its windows were shuttered, but through chinks in the slats light sprayed.

Red looked around. The street was still devoid of life. He dodged along the side of the adobe cabin. All the way around it he catfooted. It had a small back door and another small window. Red tried the door gently. It was bolted.

The window was lightly fastened too. Beyond it was blackness, probably a kitchen or bedroom.

Red could not risk breaking the window to get in. The slightest sound might warn the occupants and jeopardize his whole plan, as well as his skin. He realized there was only one thing to do.

He walked round to the front of the place again, stalked silently to the shutters. He was taking an awful chance on the street like that. He applied his eye to a lighted crack. His foolhardiness was rewarded for, after a bit of focusing, the pinched, snaggle-toothed face of the man he sought appeared in his vision.

He was sitting in a pensive attitude with his fist beneath his chin. Red manoeuvred a little to see if he could spot anyone else. His range was restricted. Anyway, if either or both of the other two men were there they were, like the runty Lafe, keeping mighty quiet.

Red moved away from the shutter and looked about him once more. Then he tiptoed swiftly to the door and lifted the latch, his other hand jerking his Colt from its sheath.

As he kicked the door open he went for his other gun too. Both of them were in his hands, levelled, waist-high as he strode into the room.

Lafe started to his feet, his mouth dropping open. He had evidently thought he had gotten away from the gaming-house quickly enough to be safe from pursuit.

'Hold it like that,' said Red, harshly. His glance swept the room as he kicked the door shut behind him. Lafe was alone.

He had got over his surprise. He leered and said,

'Howdy, pard.'

His manner infuriated the hot-blooded Red. He remembered that this was the skunk who had slugged him.

'Step away from that table,' he said. 'Then lift your gun gently an' toss it on there. Don't try any funny stuff unless you want me tuh lace you plumb up an' down the belly.'

Lafe's little eyes became wary. Red watched him like an eagle as he backed, as he reached down and lifted his gun.

'Easy now.'

The heavy Colt clattered on the table-top. Red holstered one of his own guns. Then he took three steps forward and took the one from the table. He threw it violently into a corner behind him.

He holstered his other gun then, with his hands hanging loosely, strode around the table. Immobile, only his eyes shifting, Lafe watched him.

They moved simultaneously. Red took Lafe's blow on his shoulder. His own fist crashed through the other's guard and smacked flush into the leering mouth. Lafe went over backwards.

He sat up, his hand instinctively clawing at his empty holster. His little eyes flamed murder, blood trickled from his battered lips down his pallid chin. He shook his head violently as he rose to his haunches.

Suddenly he launched himself forward, clasping Red's knees. The latter felt himself falling. He beat at the downbent head beneath him. Gosh, the fellow was fast!

Both men crashed to the floor together. Red thrust up his knees, shoving Lafe away from him. He tried to get to his feet. He was halfway there when Lafe dived again. They were both kneeling as they wrestled.

Lafe reached for one of the other's guns. He received a jolt in the midriff for his pains and recoiled with a grunt.

Red rose to his feet. He was the faster of the two this time. He waited for the other to rise. He had his adversary weighed-up now. He waited for the rush then hit Lafe again with another cruel body-blow.

Lafe jacknifed, his head forward and bent. Red uppercutted him.

Lafe crashed into a chair and went right over it. Over eager to follow up, Red in his turn sprawled headlong over the unoffending piece of furniture, which cracked heartrendingly and collapsed in sections. One of its sharp legs jabbed Red in the groin. It hurt him far more than any of Lafe's blows had done. It was also instrumental in giving the latter a brief respite.

He took it. He got to his feet at the same time as the redhead. He was a damnsight tougher than he looked. Both men advanced warily now, half-crouching, chins sunk in chests. Lafe shot out a right, then a left — like pistons. Red countered then with a cross-smother, taking the blows on elbow and forearm; his left chopped, biting into Lafe's cheek. Lafe shook his head, pressing in, jerking his knee up.

Red flinched away from the wicked thrust. He curled up his own leg and neatly hooked his adversary's. Lafe staggered. Red swung at him and missed. Lafe came forward again. Red crooked his elbow and jabbed viciously. He got savage satisfaction from the pain as the sharp bone impinged harshly on uneven buck-teeth.

Another blow on his already battered mouth seemed to send Lafe plumb crazy. His eyes blazed, he flung blows from every angle, driving Red before him. The blows the latter got in seemed to make no impression on this sudden madman.

In contrast, Red's own initial hot-temper had subsided. He got over his surprise and blocked and parried cleverly. Another terrific body-blow killed Lafe's craziness as suddenly as it had started, making him drop his fists to his middle with a gasp. Red hit him squarely in the face. He teetered away but did not fall.

The redhead was having trouble now with a nasty gash in his temple. Blood was running into his eyes. He rubbed it away with his sleeve, smearing his face until it looked like that of an Apache brave.

He was unprepared for Lafe's next onslaught. This was the most unpredictable adversary he had ever come up against! Head down he came this time, butting Red in the chest and throat. Red went down. The lithe attacker, carried along by the impetus of his own rush, sprawled on top of him, his hands clawing at his throat.

Red grasped thin, wiry wrists, tearing them away, then letting go suddenly and hitting out at the lowering, snarling face. His blows connected solidly. Lafe sprawled away from him . . .

As Red rose Lafe was waiting. He lashed out. Red took the blow, sickeningly, on his cheek bone. He went backwards across the table.

Even as Lafe's clawlike hands reached for him the redhead realized the door had opened. He tried to twist away, reaching for his left hand gun. Lafe's claw pinned his hand to the table long enough for the new arrivals to act.

Another pair of hands grasped Red's shoulders, dragging him from the table. He sprawled at the feet of Monty, the fat man. Ginger grinned in the background.

Monty let Red get to his feet and reach once more for his gun then he kicked him viciously in the kneecap. Red's breath escaped from between clenched teeth in a hiss of agony. He swung at Monty. The fat man backed away, grinning, baiting his victim.

Ignoring the pain Red made a sudden leap. The grin was wiped from Monty's face by a rock-like fist flush in his blubbery lips. He crashed into the door.

Ginger stepped forward and closed

with Red. They swapped blows. A straight left from the bank-robber sent the other redhead back into the arms of Lafe. Red's right hip became lighter as his heavy Colt was yanked from its holster. Even as he turned blue-steel flashed in the light and the barrel hit him on the side of the head. As he sank into a bottomless pit of blackness he realized that the snaggle-toothed runt had slugged him once more.

2

Butch Keaters strolled nonchalantly into El Paso's largest, wickedest saloon, The Golden Dollar. He glanced airily around him, the lamplight shining on his spectacles and giving his craggy face an almost benign look. Because of his size many glanced his way — then dismissed him as a big, harmless lummox of a cowboy and turned back to their gaming, their drinking and their women.

A red-headed percentage-girl who was well past the age of innocence sidled up to him with a 'Hi-yuh, big boy.'

'Hi-yuh, beautiful,' said Butch mechanically and passed on.

There was so much smoke, he could barely discern the far corners of the room. He reached the bar and ordered a drink from one of the four barmen. Resting his foot on the brass-rail, he half-turned, his hand dangling, though seemingly unconsciously, close to the butt of his lowslung gun. It was then he saw Slip.

The lean younker was lounging unobtrusively against the wall. From this cunningly-selected vantage-point he could survey the whole of the room. Also nobody could get up to him without his seeing them.

To the left of him was the dais on which a pianist, a fiddler and a guitar-player ground out garbled rhythms for the benefit of the couples who shuffled on the small space of floor cleared for this purpose. Slip wasn't picketed there because he liked music or bunny-hugging, nor was it a coincidence that at the other side of him was the little side-door of The Golden Dollar.

Good ol' Slip. Butch had too much sense then to approach his colleague openly.

Slip spotted him. His dark face did not change expression. Butch inclined his head gently in the direction of the door. Then he turned back to his drink.

He did not look in Slip's direction again but a little later strolled noncha-lantly outside. He moved away from the bright lights and leaned against a hitching-post. He rolled a cigarette and lit up. He had dragged away at half of it when Slip joined him.

Four men passed them. 'Howdy,' said Slip gruffly.

There was a chorus of 'Howdys' from men inclined to be friendly now rather than suspicious. They passed on with-out another glance.

Butch handed over the makings. Slip

rolled himself a quirly and lit up. Butch waited till his pard's smoke was going strong then he drawled.

'Wal, did you see anythin' or find out anythin'?'

'I didn't see anythin' or find out anythin',' drawled Slip in his turn. 'The folks here shut up like clams if you ask 'em the right time . . . Where's Red?'

'I left him in a gambling house about half an hour ago. I've bin browzin' around. I ain't seen or heard anythin' either. The town's full of owlhooters but I ain't had a smell of our three friends.'

'Wal, if yuh left Red in a gambling-house I guess he'll still be there. What say we find him then go get some shut-eye?'

'It wasn't my idea to come out in the first place,' grumbled Butch.

'All right, ol' timer,' said Slip with a hint of levity in his voice. 'We shall not linger much longer. Let's go get him. Where is he?'

'Just down the street a piece,' grunted

Butch, unmollified. He led the way, lumbering pompously along the board-walk. Slip catfooted behind him.

Butch halted outside the half-open door of the gaming-house.

'This is it,' he said. 'You go in an' get him.'

Slip slid past him and through the door. Butch lit another smoke and ambled on a little way. Presently Slip joined him.

'He's not there,' he said.

'Not there?' echoed Butch. 'Wal, ain't that somethin'? What's he doin' — reforming?'

'Maybe he dropped a packet,' said Slip. 'An' he's reconnoitring for more. I guess we'd better look for him before he gets too much likker inside of him. We don't want to hafta leave this town in a hurry. That ain't in the plans at all.'

'Nope,' said Butch. 'C'mon . . . Oh my pore achin' body,' he groaned.

'Yuh got too much of it,' quipped his lean partner. As unobtrusively as possible they ranged the nightspots of

El Paso. Where there were brawls they looked for Red. When he was liquored-up he loved a fight. They did not find him. Finally Butch said: 'Maybe he's gone back to the rooming-house.'

'Yeh, maybe,' said Slip. 'We'll go back.'

'If he's back there poundin' his ear I swear I'll have his ginger scalp,' vowed Butch.

The rooming-house was quiet. In the lobby the seemingly tireless Pop was still at his post. It seemed he looked at them a mite queerly as they entered.

As they crossed to the foot of the stairs, the pimply-faced young runabout came through a door. When he spotted them his pale eyes bugged out from his head. He backed hesitantly then suddenly made a dash past them to the stairs.

Butch grabbed the slack at the back of his trousers. 'What's eatin' you, sonny?' he growled.

The kid gave a half-strangled squeal

72

of sheer terror. Boots thudded on the landing up above.

'They're here!' screamed the kid.

Two men appeared suddenly at the top of the stairs. The youth snatched himself wildly away from Butch and like a trapped hare seeking escape crashed into the stair-rail.

Both men upstairs went for their guns. Moving surprisingly fast for his bulk Butch leapt sideways. He knew he could depend on Slip to look out for himself.

Even as he drew, firing from the hip, he heard the blatter of the younker's twin Colts in his ears.

With a hoarse cry the foremost of the two men came headlong down the stairs. At the same time the pimply-faced kid screamed horribly and reeled away, clutching his side. He had stopped a shot slung by one of the surprised deputies upstairs.

Slip stood, legs apart, both guns out. He fired again as the man upstairs backed into the shadows. The man retaliated as his pard rolled at Slip's feet. Slip's hat spun from his head. He dodged with Butch into the shadows beside the stairs.

The fallen man, who had only been slightly wounded in the leg, rose suddenly, swinging up his gun.

White teeth bared, Slip shot him coolly betwcen the eyes. Simultaneously, with a well-placed shot, Butch smashed a glass on Pop's desk as the old man reached for the shotgun on hooks in the wall behind him. The palsied hands dropped.

'Come out here, Pop,' said Butch, as Slip reloaded quickly.

The old man came out from behind his desk and bent over his moaning young side-kick who was crumpled up against it.

Upstairs sobbing gasps revealed that the other deputy had been hit.

'I'm goin' up there,' hissed Slip. 'Look out.'

He leapt suddenly to the bottom step, both guns blazing. Behind this veritable curtain of lead he ran upwards.

The deputy, his one leg shattered, dragged himself desperately along the passage. He turned as Slip reached the top of the stairs.

The lean man slung himself forward, flat on his belly, his one gun held outward straight, and blazing. Slugs fanned his hair.

The deputy coughed horribly and crumpled slowly to a still shapeless mass in the darkness.

Slip passed through a haze of gunsmoke, jumped over the body, and flung open the door of their room. It was empty.

'Slip,' called Butch urgently.

He ran downstairs again. From out in the street came a clamour of voices.

'Red ain't there,' said Slip.

'Out the back way,' said Butch. He grabbed Pop's shotgun from its hook and led the way.

They passed through the door and found themselves among the ashcans and refuse of the back.

'We gotta find Red,' said Slip.

'Yeh, but let's get away from this first. Red's got more sense than tuh try to get into the rooming-house while all that activity's goin' on.'

Half-crouching, swerving to avoid dark miscellaneous objects which bestrewed their path, they blundered onwards.

# 4

## 1

Red McGrath opened his eyes slowly, shook his head to dispel the bloodshot haze that encompassed him. Stabs of pain shot through his skull. He raised himself on his elbow, his other hand mechanically reaching for his gun. He was surprised to find it still in its holster.

He raised himself into a sitting position, looking around him, trying to fix his eyes on something concrete in a swimming universe in which he was carried along on wave after wave of throbbing pain. Vaguely he realized he was still in the adobe cabin, the lamp was still lit. As his vision became clearer he realized also that he was alone. He reached for his other gun. The holster was empty.

He spotted the gun on the floor a little way away from him. He crawled across and got hold of it. With painful concentration he placed it in its rightful position. The successful accomplishment of this feat made him feel a whole lot better. But he still felt as if he had spent the last few days on the back of a killer stallion and had been finally tossed off on his head.

With a mighty effort which sent agony screaming through him he rose to his feet. He staggered to the table, held on, then, from there, flopped into a convenient chair.

He surveyed the room again. The door was shut, the place was strangely bare: the overturned splintered chair, a shattered glass on the table, not much else — after beating Red up, the three bankrobbers had high-tailed it pretty quickly. They had even left their victim's guns behind — under the assumption no doubt that he wouldn't be in a fit state to use them yet awhile anyway.

Red took the weapons from their sheaths and placed them on the table before him. Then he picked them up again one by one and spun the cylinders expertly, handling the sleek oily steel and the ribbed walnut butts with loving fingers. From now on these Colts were pledged to blast the life from three men, who, in Red's estimation, were better dead anyhow.

He felt a heap better. He holstered the guns, rising to his feet. He skirted the table and, reaching upwards, unhooked the hurricane lantern from the ceiling. Holding this before him he pushed open the door which led into the back room and crossed the threshold.

This place was pretty bare, too: two cots with tumbled bedclothes, a small table on which reposed a bowl of dirty water, a hanging cupboard on the wall. Most probably the three desperadoes had hired the cabin for a short while from the gent who owned it.

Red opened the cupboard. There was

half-a-loaf, a can of peaches, a bag of sugar, and, wonders of wonders, a bottle of whiskey.

Red took a swig. It made his throbbing head sing but filled his belly with fire and new life.

He went back into the other room. He blew out the lamp, put it on the table. He crossed the room, opened the outer door and peered out. The little backwater was still deserted. He stepped out and closed the door softly behind him. His knees felt like water but he steeled himself to walk as jauntily as possible down the street.

He had nearly reached its end when a man came out of a log-hut and looked at him suspiciously. 'Howdy,' said Red cheerily. The man grunted a surly reply then began to walk in the opposite direction. Red willed himself not to look round, not to appear curious.

He passed through a dark gap between larger buildings and so into the main street — and into signs of activity that were not present the last time he passed along there.

People were hurrying about. Some of them were even running. Nobody paid much heed to Red as he limped along in the shadows. Unobtrusively he followed the bulk of the crowd who all seemed to be going in the same direction — the direction that he had meant to follow himself. Now curiosity and a strange foreboding impelled him forward.

He reached the Golden Dollar saloon and mingled with the folks who issued therefrom. Only then did he hear the news that was passed from lip to lip. Shootings were common in El Paso but this was a particularly sensational one . . . Two of Marshall Max Winters deputies — shot deader'n mackerel — by two wanted men — bank-robbers — down at Pop's rooming-house — killers got away.

Red paused, his brain racing, his pain and tiredness almost entirely swept away from him by this sudden revelation. He slipped away from the crowd,

81

reconstructing in his mind what he knew must have happened. He knew Butch and Slip wouldn't leave town without him. They'd be looking for him — even as the mob would be looking for them. He must try and find them himself — but carefully for fear of giving them away.

Red limped up an alley to the backs of the buildings and began to work his way along in the direction of the rooming-house. He climbed fences and tumbled over rubbish and timber. There were other people beside himself scouting around there, shafts of light spilled from back windows, men called to each other.

Red bumped into a small bunch of people. 'I thought I saw somethin' movin' over there,' he said excitedly pointing to where the first weedy fringes of the range backed into town.

They went with him and in the darkness he broke away from them again. He dodged into the darkness of a small tumbledown lean-to as another large bunch came along.

'Spread out in threes,' said a deep authoritative voice. 'Don't git shootin' at shadows.'

Marshal Max Winters had arrived on the scene and the town was getting organized for a manhunt. Red knew, however, that to organize such a chase in a town like this was far from easy: it was quite probable that innocent blood would be shed by over-eager trigger-jerkers before the night was out.

He made a short detour around the back of Pop's place — although he figured people wouldn't look for the killers so near the scene of their crime. He figured also that maybe Slip and Butch would be thinking just that.

He finished up by the small stables which housed the horses of himself and his friends. He stepped into the pitch-darkness and whistled softly a few bars of his favourite Spanish serenade.

'Red,' hissed a voice immediately. 'Up here. Hi'st yourself up.'

Red's eyes were now becoming

accustomed to the darkness. He looked upwards to the small loft, seeing only the hay that spilled over its sides. Then a head appeared.

'Don't stand there gapin',' hissed a peevish voice. 'Shin up that pillar.'

Painfully Red hauled himself up by one of the stall-pillars. Butch's hands grasped him and pulled him up among the hay between himself and the silent Slip.

'This was the only place I figured I might find yuh.'

'You figured right. We doubled back. They came in here to see if our hosses wuz gone but they never thought of lookin' up here.'

'Lucky for them.' Slip spoke suddenly, grimly, lifting his hands and showing the blue-steel barrels of his twin Colts. Then he left Butch and Red to it again.

They did not waste time but told their respective stories briefly.

Then Butch said: 'How're things outside? D'yuh think we can make a break for it?'

'Yeh, they seem to be movin' like you figured, up tuh the other end o' town. We oughta be able to ride plumb out of here and right on tuh the range.'

'Let's git goin' then,' chimed-in Slip. He wriggled to the edge, let himself over then dropped with a soft thud. Red and Butch followed suit.

They saddled-up swiftly. Red cat-footed to the door.

'Nobody right near,' he said. 'A lot o' yelling and moving about a bit lower down. We might get spotted but we'll have a start. Climb on, I'll swing the door open.' He did so, then ran back and mounted his own horse.

Butch went first, then Slip; Red came last. As they left the door they urged their horses into a gallop. They lay flat in their saddles, their heads behind the horses' necks.

As they left the hard soil and hit the first fringe of the grasslands somebody shouted. Shots echoed above the steady thudding of their horses hooves, a couple of slugs whined pretty close.

The shotgun guard of the long distance stage between Stockton and El Paso was a very cautious *hombre*. He was always particularly vigilant as the four-horse coach rumbled through Snake Pass on the last lap of its journey — for this narrow, dark cleft in a wild, craggy country was a stick-up man's dream. Not that there *had* been a hold-up there for twelve months or more.

The last one, due to the vigilance of the aforesaid guard, was from the point of view of the stick-up men, a tragic fiasco. One of them was shot dead, the other escaped but was picked up the same day and subsequently given a stretch in the State pen.

Ever since then the guard, with a 'let-'em-all come' attitude, had been doubly vigilant — sort of balancing a chip on his shoulder and daring any get-rich-quick merchant to try and knock it off.

The day they carried the first pay-roll for the El Paso railway-workers he rode for a fall. He never had a chance . . .

Ginger was the brains of the outfit. He planned the coup. And he made sure of the guard right away by picking him off coolly from cover with a Sharps rifle.

The driver didn't need a second hint. He dived from his perch and sought cover on the ground at the other side of the coach. Monty, from his position in cover at that side of the road shot him in the back before he even had a chance to lift his gun.

A male passenger in the coach opened up at Monty who kept well in cover until his two pards had a chance to get down.

Then Ginger yelled: 'You're covered from both sides, folks. Better climb down an' look happy unless you all want to get kilt.'

From the interior of the coach tumbled a dumb-looking Easterner in broadcloth, a middle-aged woman, a beautiful younger one, a frail-looking boy who seemed more intrigued than scared, and a tall man in Western garb who slung his gun roughly at the feet of Ginger and Lafe.

'I don't want the ladies or the boy hurt,' he said.

'That's mighty sensible of you, friend,' said Ginger. 'Now jest reach for your wallet too.'

The tall man reached inside his vest and brought forth a billfold. This he tossed savagely at their feet too.

'Mighty disrespectful ain't yuh?' snarled Ginger. 'Now pick it up and hand it over nicely like a good boy.' The tall man stuck his chin out and stubbornly stood his ground.

Ginger's thin lips curled with passion, revealing stumpy yellow teeth.

'Pick it up,' he said more softly. 'Or I'll shoot yuh in the belly an' make yuh crawl to it.'

It was obvious to all present that he meant what he said. The Westerner took a few paces forward and bent his long body. His hand reached for the wallet. He was very close to Lafe. He acted swiftly, his body uncoiling again, springing at Lafe's middle. But Ginger was quicker. His gun swung in an arc, descended with sickening force on the back of the man's head. He fell full length without a sound.

The Easterner in broadcloth was not as dumb as he looked. Nor did he lack courage. He drew a small snub-nosed automatic suddenly from inside his coat. But he was not fast enough to beat these men who lived by the gun. It was Lafe who shot him. His eyes staring, his mouth gaping, he vainly tried to raise his gun. He crumpled in a heap.

The two women and the boy stood rooted by terror, their eyes glazed.

Lafe turned the body over, fished callously in the clothing and brought forth a bulky wallet. He handed this to Ginger.

From his perch on the coach, where he had been rummaging in the boot beneath the driver's seat, Monty called: 'It ain't here.'

'Look inside the coach,' snarled Ginger.

Monty clambered laboriously down. The sun glinted on the lens of the steel-rimmed spectacles he wore. He got inside the coach.

'Here it is,' he said and came forth again holding an attaché-case.

'Open it,' said Ginger.

'It's locked.'

'Stand out o' the way then.'

Monty did so. Ginger levelled his gun and fired. The case was lifted from the ground as the heavy slug smashed into the lock. The lid flew open, revealing an interior packed tightly with green bills.

'Git the hosses, Lafe,' said Ginger.

The snaggle-toothed runt did as he was told. Ginger tied the loaded attaché-case in front of his own saddle. The three men mounted.

'So-long, ladies,' Ginger jeered. They put spurs to their horses and galloped down the hard dry, sunbaked road in a cloud of white dust.

The tall Westerner groaned and rolled over.

The women ran to him and helped him into a sitting position.

'The skunks!' he said. Weakly he tried to rise, but couldn't quite make it. He sank back with a groan of despair.

'Rest awhile,' said the beautiful young woman. 'You can't do anything now anyway. They've gotten clean away.'

What she said, although she did not know it, was not strictly true. The three killers did *not* get clean away. Fate, or whatever deity ordains such things, played a little trick on them. It was but a small penalty and ultimately was the means of bringing about the death at their hands of yet another innocent person. Yet, undoubtedly, it was another link to the chain of their evil destinies.

When they got out of sight of the coach and its stricken occupants round the bend of the road, the three men left the trail and made tracks across the grassland. They were going good and beginning to compliment themselves on the simplicity of making a living the owl-hoot way when Ginger's mare put her foot in a gopher hole. The beast gave a whinney of pain and pitched forward, throwing the rider over its head.

Ginger fell awkwardly. When he rose he was grunting with pain, his left hand hanging awkwardly.

'My wrist's busted,' he said.

The horse lay still on its side, its liquid eyes rolling in agony. 'Do something,' snarled Ginger. His face was white as he nursed his injured fin.

Lafe dismounted, produced a red bandanna and tied the wrist up, pulling the knot so tightly that Ginger cursed him.

'It's busted proper,' said Lafe. 'It wants fixin'.'

'Don't I know it,' snarled Ginger.

Meanwhile fat Monty was bending over the horse.

'Her leg's busted up,' he said.

'Try to get her to her feet,' said Ginger.

Monty said to Lafe: 'Gimme a hand . . . I guess it ain't much use tho'.'

Between them they hauled the beast to her feet. The broken limb gave way beneath her. They let her fall again. She lay, looking up at them piteously.

Ginger cursed madly and drew his gun. From where he stood he pumped three slugs into the mare's head.

'You're the lightest, Lafe,' he said. 'I'll get up behind you.'

The other two re-mounted. Ginger handed the battered attaché-case up to Lafe and climbed up behind him. The redhead was sweating with pain.

'Can't afford tuh waste time,' he said through clenched teeth. 'Git goin'. We gotta get to the nearest town so's I can get this wrist fixed and find another hoss.'

## 3

Doc Trapps of Scarsville was a wizened baldheaded old coot with sleepy eyes who was a darnsight wilier than he looked. He was well-loved in this little cowtown which had been his home for thirty-five years. He was everybody's doctor and everybody's friend.

He was hotheaded: a fighter, but a righteous one. When men came to him with gunshot wounds he liked to know where they got 'em. But he never refused to treat anybody. That was why when a fat man with spectacles confronted him with a drawn gun and asked for treatment for his red-headed friend's broken wrist Doc Trapps said gently:

'You don't need the hardware, friend. It's my job to mend busted wrists.'

'We got no time tuh chew the fat,' said Ginger harshly. He extended his arm. 'Get on with it.'

The doc looked a harmless and rather dumb old jackass. Monty let his gun dangle while Ginger's wrist was fitted up fine and dandy — sling and all.

'Thanks, doc,' said Ginger with a sneer in his voice. He motioned to his friend. They turned to go, Monty with the gun still dangling carelessly in his hand.

Doc Trapps was a hornery old cuss; he didn't like being taken advantage of.

He said: 'Before you gentlemen go I wish you'd tell me why you're in such an all-fired hurry and why you think a gun is necessary when you enter a doctor's surgery?'

Both men turned to look into the barrel of a huge Frontier model Colt which had appeared in the doc's hand as if by magic.

'Drop the gun, fat man,' said the doc.

Monty, his mouth agape, dropped his gun with a clatter.

Ginger gave him a glare of baffled rage. Then he turned to the old man.

'Look, doc, we're in a hurry.'

'Yeh, I gathered that much.'

Ginger moved a little nearer. Monty followed.

'Wal, doc, we'll tell yuh . . . '

'You've come quite near enough to do so,' said the old man.

The two men stopped. They had achieved their aim and moved away from the door, which was slightly ajar. It was flung wide open violently, and Lafe, who had been standing lookout outside, fired two rapid shots.

The old man did not have a chance, the heavy slugs knocked him over backwards.

'C'mon,' said Lafe.

The other two followed him. A figure appeared in their path. Lafe fired again. The figure went down but rose so far to clasp Monty, who brought up the rear, around the knees. The fat man savagely kicked aside the troublesome encumbrance and lumbered on.

Ginger had managed to steal another horse. He mounted awkwardly. The other two followed suit. Before the townsfolk of Scarsville had little more time than to merely speculate on the origin of the two shots they were galloping out of town. Little did those same townsfolk realize that those sudden shots they heard at twilight were to herald a night of tragedy unprecedented in their annals, which, judged by the standards of the times and territory they lived in had been fairly peaceable till now.

The youth who had been slightly wounded by Lafe's shot as the three men fled, rose to his feet and with one hand clapped tightly to his bleeding thigh limped through the open door of Doc Trapp's place.

'Doc,' he croaked and went down beside the still form. But the old man was dead; his frail chest had been smashed by the heavy slugs.

The fifteen-year old youth, Benny, known to almost everybody as Doc's boy, was an orphan and had been the old bachelor's virtual son as well as general factotum as long as he could remember. He realized that death would have to part them sometime but he had not expected it to happen so soon, so suddenly, and in such a terrible way.

He was sobbing brokenly as he limped out into the street. Folks were coming from all directions now. Two men caught the boy as he fell.

# 5

## 1

Sheriff Abel Kent, of Scarsville, learnt from the incoherent ravings of the sick and grief-stricken Benny that there had been three men and the one he grabbed had been a big man who wore glasses. The huge man with the glasses that shone in the light from the open doorway had become a terrible figure of nightmare to the boy.

The old sheriff's troubled grief-ridden features (John Trapps had been his best friend) became more haggard as he listened. He thought of the Wanted notice that was pinned up in his office — the notice that had caused him so much worry already.

He told his two deputies to stay in town and then he quickly formed a posse, which he meant to take out himself. But his plan was forestalled by yet another occurrence, another link in the tragic chain which was to make the little cow town of Scarsville as notorious as El Paso or the infamous Tombstone.

A four-horse coach came rumbling and swaying at breakneck speed down the single dusty main street. The crowd outside the sheriff's office scattered in all directions as with a screeching of steel on its wheels it drew to a standstill. A tall dishevelled man in conventional Western garb leapt from its seat, followed by a white-faced boy. The coach-door opened and from its interior came a motherly-looking middle-aged lady and a younger lady with hair the colour of the morning sunlight and a look of sadness clouding the smooth beauty of her face.

The tall man said rapidly: 'We've been held up an' robbed. Three men killed. This was the nearest town. The killers seemed to come this way. Three of 'em.'

'They've been . . . and gone,' said Sheriff Kent sombrely.

'The driver, the guard and a gentleman from back East — all killed,' said the tall man. 'They're in the coach. Will somebody give me a hand?'

There were many anxious volunteers. Onlookers surveyed the two women that had travelled in a coach with three dead bodies.

The tall man said: 'The driver lived for a while. Mrs Bullock here and Miss Calthorpe are nurses. They did all they could but it was hopeless from the start.'

The three bodies were carried into the undertaker's just down the street. The tall man, the two ladies, and the boy, followed Sheriff Kent into his office. He shut out the crowd. He turned to his deputies.

'You'd better go out in my place. You know what to do. Take all the men you can an' split 'em up. Go on, get movin'.'

The two men obeyed, grimly and with alacrity.

101

The tall man told the story and introduced himself as Jack Berners of Stockton. He was an agent for the railroad. The payroll the bandits had taken had been in his charge. The boy was his nephew, Tim, who he was bringing West with him for his health.

The two nurses, Mrs Bullock, widow of a railwayman, and Miss Ann Calthorpe, were going to El Paso to set up a small hospital there — a commendable, courageous, and in all probability, a difficult task.

The dead man from back East had been Mr George Kipton, of Chicago. What his intended business in the West had been Berners did not know. He only knew that the man had had guts.

'You had a good look at the bandits?' said Sheriff Kent.

'We all did,' said Berners. 'I'd know them anyplace.'

The ladies agreed they would too. 'So would I,' said young Tim doggedly. Despite his frailness he seemed pretty cool for a young 'un.

'I only want to meet up with 'em again,' said Berners grimly. 'I'm ready tuh ride with you anytime you say, sheriff. Right now is as good a time as any.'

'I've sent a posse out,' said the sheriff. 'My deputies are good men — experienced trackers. Anyway, Mr Berners, what you want is a night's rest before you'll be fit tuh do any hard riding. That's a nasty crack you had on your head.'

'I guess you're right, sheriff,' said Berners. 'I do feel kinda groggy now yuh come tuh mention it.'

'I suggest you and the lad go and see Pete Jimsin at his rooming-house down the street,' said the sheriff. 'I haven't got room for all of yuh at my place but I can find enough room for the two ladies.'

'That's very kind of you, sheriff,' said Mrs Bullock. 'If you're sure . . . '

'My wife and myself will be very glad to have you,' said the lawman gravely. 'I'll take you there right away.'

103

He escorted the two ladies to his frame bungalow where his buxom wife, Marie, welcomed them with open arms. The sheriff did not stay himself but returned to the office. His was to be a long and anxious night. Little did he know that he was to have another surprise before the dawn broke.

He had just returned from viewing the bodies of the victims of the stage robbery and also seeing that of his old friend, John Trapps, gently laid-out by Simon Greave, the undertaker, when the back door of his office opened and three men entered.

'Hallo, Abel,' said the foremost; big, tough-looking, wearing spectacles. Behind him slouched a long, lean dark young man.

The sheriff drew his gun. 'Keep your distance, boys,' he said.

Butch said: 'Red's hurt.'

Slip said: 'I guess we don't blame yuh after seein' that Wanted notice on the wall.' He stepped to one side. Red McGrath staggered in, turned, and slumped down on the bench against the wall.

His face was pale and drawn beneath its tan and the dirt which streaked it. His red hair straggled from under his hat, he was unkept and tattered. Sheriff Kent had difficulty in recognizing in him the devil-may-care, rather dandified young man who had been one of his deputies not so very long ago.

The sheriff was bewildered, he looked from Red to his two pards, then back again. He still held his gun.

Slip said: 'Yuh must know yuh've got the wrong pigeons, Abel.'

The old man blurted out: 'John Trapps was shot and killed by three men tonight, one of 'em a big feller with glasses. Earlier than that the Stockton-El Paso coach was held up by the same men — three men killed . . .'

Totally ignoring the sheriff's gun Butch started forward. 'Doc Trapps — kilt — how, when?'

Mechanically the sheriff jerked the gun. Butch stopped dead. 'Abel . . .'

'Sit down,' said the old man. 'Sit by Red both of yuh. Stay put.'

He backed towards the door and opened it. People were still lounging around the stage-coach. Speculating, inspecting, gossiping.

'Come here some of yuh!' yelled the sheriff.

There were quite a few volunteers. The sheriff gave hurried instructions. Then he closed the door. He turned back to the three men.

Slip said: 'Red's plenty knocked-up. He took a beatin' at El Paso — yuh know what a one he is for fightin'. Ever since then we've been hounded by a skunk called Max Winters and a pack o' men, and haven't had chance to rest.'

'I've sent for somebody tuh tend tuh Red,' said Kent.

Slip, talkative for once, continued. 'I guess we've managed to shake the skunk off at last.' He grinned mirthlessly 'Anyway, he'll hardly expect tuh find us here . . .'

'For Pete's sake, Abel,' interrupted

Butch suddenly. 'Point that gun some-
place else. You know us.'

The old sheriff looked uncertain, his
face was clouded with worry. But he
held on to the gun. 'Carry on with your
story,' he said.

Slip talked on. It was the longest
speech either of the other three men
had ever heard him make. Beginning
where Red shot the gambler at the
gaming-table he told the whole story.

Butch interjected remarks from time
to time. Red sat silent, his head bent.
Once or twice he looked up and
seemed to smile to himself at Slip's
witticisms, which were usually directed
at him. The colour seemed to be
returning to his face.

There came a knock at the door.
'Come in,' said the sheriff.

It opened and a vision of loveliness
appeared. The old mahogany tan
returned to Red's handsome, though
now rather battered visage.

'This is Miss Calthorpe,' said the
sheriff. 'She's a nurse. Better let her

have a look at you, son.'

'I feel a whole lot better already,' said Red and grinned at the vision.

She smiled. 'Will you come over here by the light, please?' she said.

Red rose. The sheriff waved his gun.

'Jest a minute. I'd like to ask Miss Calthorpe a question.'

'What's that, Mr Kent?' said the girl.

'Have you ever seen these men before?'

'No, I haven't . . . ' Then the girl laughed, a delicious sound. 'Though I will admit that when I first came in and saw the gentleman in the spectacles, I thought . . . well, you know what I thought, sheriff. Now I know I was entirely mistaken. Although it is rather a coincidence don't you think — a big man with spectacles, though he isn't I think, so fat . . . and a man with auburn hair. The other one was I think smaller than the dark young man . . . '

'Yeh,' said Kent. Then he sighed audibly and lowered his gun. His face was puckered as he said haltingly:

'I'm sorry, boys. You wuz allus kinda wild . . . Then the Wanted notice . . . yuh understand . . . I'm glad it's all right — plumb glad. It was just that . . . '

'Forget it, Abel,' said Butch. Then he grinned hugely. 'You allus was a suspicious ol' cuss . . . ' Boot heels thudded outside the office and the door was rapped again. The sheriff called 'Come in' and a tall man entered.

He stopped dead in his tracks. His hand flew to his hip. Then he slapped his thigh.

'Gosh!' he said. 'For a moment I thought . . . '

'This is Mr Berners of Stockton, boys,' said the sheriff. 'He brought the stage in. Mr Berners — my ex-deputies.'

The tall man, he even towered above Slip and Butch, shook hands around. Red moved across the room to the golden-haired girl and for the next few minutes he was in a dream of bliss while, with a first-aid pack, she treated him for sundry cuts and bruises.

'What you need most,' she said 'is plenty of rest.'

'I feel fine,' burbled Red and became inarticulate again, swimming away in her beautiful blue eyes.

Some time later they all left the office, the five men to go to the undertaker's parlour, the girl back to the sheriff's house. Red, always the gallant, wanted to see her home, but was joked out of it by his pards.

A few minutes later he was standing silently with the others seeing his old friend, Doc Trapps for the last time. 'You knew him well?' said Berners softly.

It was Butch who answered for them all.

'Yeh we knew him well . . . He gave me these glasses,' he added. He took them off and began to polish them slowly, mechanically, a sign that he was under stress of emotion, a sign that boded ill for somebody.

The three partners got lodgings with dried-up, jolly little Mrs Flaherty, an old friend of theirs who kept a rooming-house in the main street. They awoke just after dawn and after breakfast went to the sheriff's office. They learnt that the posse had not yet returned.

Old Abel had spent a sleepless night waiting for his men and, hopefully, their captives. Or at least news of some kind.

Butch said: 'Abel, ol' hoss, we hereby swear ourselves in as your deputies again. You get off home right away an' get some shut-eye. We'll look after this end. You know you can depend on us.'

The sheriff, a stickler for duty, hummed and hawed for a bit but was finally prevailed upon to do as they suggested. After he had left them time passed slowly. Red wanted to call on the ravishing golden-haired Miss Calthrope but was told sternly by the other two that now he was a full-blown deputy once more he had no time for gallivanting. Red was a new man this morning. He just grinned blissfully. He could wait.

Under the boys' light-hearted banter, however, was a feeling of tension. They were eager for action: it irked them to be hanging about here while the murderers of one of their best friends, the same evil men who had caused them so much trouble, were maybe getting away scot-free.

What irked Butch most of all was the fact that the fat Monty had begun sporting a pair of spectacles. The three killers were really passing the buck on to the partners now. Little did they know what unholy delight Ginger got from this little scheme of his.

Halfway through the morning a disgruntled and weary posse returned empty-handed. The miscreants had gotten away somewhere over the Mexican border. Right now American law could not touch them. As one of the posse hotly put it: first of all there'd have tuh be a lot of bowing and scraping to stinking greasers, while the killers got further and further away. They had enough cash now to go anywhere they pleased.

'There's more'n one kind o' justice,' said Butch grimly as the members of the posse went away to get a meal and a rest.

'Yeh,' said Slip, catching his drift. 'I guess this is the time to resign from being deputies.'

'Mighty short term of office,' said Red, but there was no mirth in his tone.

The three men began to make plans but were interrupted by a knock on the door.

'Come in,' said Butch.

The door was opened and Miss Ann Calthorpe entered. 'Good morning,' she said and asked for news. She expressed regret at the bad tidings when they told her of them. Then she asked after the health of her erstwhile patient.

'Couldn't be better,' said Red. 'You

did wonders with me last night.' Then he dried up. This girl seemed to hold the reins on his usually glib tongue.

'Sit down,' she said. 'Let me have a look at you again.'

Red obeyed with alacrity and while she ministered to him looked blissfully up into her blue eyes. She smiled and he beamed foolishly. Doubtless, being a nurse, she was used to such behaviour on the part of her male patients.

Finally the reins became slack on Red's tongue again. He said: 'How long you figuring to stay in Scarsville, Miss Calthorpe?'

'I can't really say, Mr McGrath,' she said. 'Mrs Kent says we are welcome to stay at her house as long as we wish. I — I'd like to see those murderers brought to justice . . .'

'It may take months now, Miss Calthorpe.'

'Yes — I know. Mrs Bullock wants to go on to El Paso in a few days . . . I guess there's nothing else we can do here. Mr Berners has asked us to take young Tim with us and hand him over to a friend of his on the railroad there.'

'Why, is Mr Berners going some-place?' asked Red warily.

'I guess he wants to help out here as long as he can.' The girl moved away a little. She had finished.

Red stood up. He was bolder now. He said: 'I guess we'll be ridin' ourselves purty soon. I'd like to call an' say so-long before we go.'

They were no longer nurse and patient now. As this handsome young man with the level grey eyes stood looking at her with undisguised admiration Ann Calthorpe lost her professional poise.

She said rather haltingly. 'I'll be at the Kent place.' Then with a hurried good-morning to the other two men and a last fleeting glance at the smiling Red, she left the office.

'Oh, gosh,' said Red and sat down again.

Butch and Slip exchanged meaning glances and grinned.

Slip said: 'Snap out of it, Romeo. Come over here an' look at this map. We gotta try an' figure where them killers might be making for.'

Red lounged to the desk and joined them.

'I'm rarin' tuh go,' he said.

Slip stabbed the map with a lean forefinger. 'About there is where the posse lost 'em,' he said. 'It's all wild, rocky country — a sort of an outcrop from the Sierra Madre — lotta ghost-towns an' little settlements — real bandit country . . . D'yuh remember how Lopez Red and his cutthroats useter raid the border-towns from up there a couple or three years ago?'

'Yeah,' said Butch. 'Gosh, if them ginks are holing-up in that territory we'll have a heck of a job tuh find 'em.'

'We'll find 'em,' said Red.

'Unless they're ridin' right across Mexico,' said Butch.

'Somehow I don't think so,' said Slip. 'There's nothin' across that county tuh interest three Americans. If I wuz them I'd hole up till the storm blows over then come back into the States an' make fer the East.'

'Hopin' meanwhile three other *hombres* had been strung-up instead of 'em,' said Red. 'I guess you're right. I vote we ride up there pronto.'

'After the funeral,' said Butch.

'Yeh, *right* after the funeral.'

That afternoon Doc Trapps was being laid to rest in Boot Hill, where so many of his friends had gone before him. Wherever he went he would never be lonely.

The whole town turned out to pay tribute to his memory. The burial service was held at the little tin chapel. The sun blazed and the sweat poured from the faces of the congregation as Ep Lomas, the sky-pilot, another great friend of the doc's, gave one of the most sincere spiels of his history. Those of the townsfolk who couldn't get into the confines of the tin tabernacle, and they were the luckiest, clustered outside and waited. Despite the heat, the flies and the discomfort, there was genuine feeling by the majority. Doc Trapps had been a pretty lovable old cuss.

Finally the service was over and the bearers, Butch, Red, Slip and Sheriff Kent, carried the coffin outside and followed by the small multitude began to carry it up the hill to the cemetery. It was a real old Western funeral, with the dead man's best friends carrying him all the way to his last resting-place, and all the rest of them pacing slowly behind.

As the population massed on Boot Hill a band of horsemen rode in at the other end of town. They might have been riding into a ghost-town. They halted, puzzled.

At their head rode a big man whose raven-black hair flowed from beneath a black Mexican sombrero and whose hawk-like face was as dark and as cruel as an Indian's. The illusion was only dispelled by a thread of moustache on his upper lip, a thing that no real Indian would ever wear. The man's shirt was a vivid blue, his neckerchief red. He wore a heavy gun-belt and two Colts were strapped in a very businesslike manner to his lusty, chap-covered thighs.

His men, about a dozen of them in all, were a motley-looking bunch. They all looked hard and reckless, men who lived hair-trigger lives, disreputable epitomes of the Western dogma of survival of the fittest.

They rode on, then, at a sign from their leader, dismounted outside the nearest saloon and hitched their horses to the rail.

The sleepy-eyed bartender jerked bolt upright at the sudden invasion of his premises.

The big man ordered drinks all round. After the barman had seen to the order the big man said to him 'Where is everybody in this pesky town?'

The man had got over his surprise. He replied laconically: 'A funeral up at Boot Hill.'

'He must've been a real popular guy, the one they're buryin'.'

'He was.'

The men dispersed themselves around the saloon and drank and smoked and talked. After a short while the big man left the bar and moved amongst them. Those he spoke to left the saloon, nonchalantly. Once outside they quickened their pace and started up the street: one man alone, then a pair, then another pair on the other side of the street. All keeping close to the buildings as they moved along the boardwalk. As they began to climb gently, the mourners came into view descending the slope from Boot Hill — leaving behind them for the last time the man who had helped them and ministered to them for so long. In their environment, where dog-eat-dog was the paramount maxim, sentiment was rare. But now that emotion was awakened in most breasts and nobody took any notice of the unobtrusive strangers in the street.

Butch, Red, Slip and Sheriff Kent went into the office. The rest carried on to the saloon to forget, as is time-honoured, with plenty of liquor.

The sheriff closed the door. 'So you're ridin', boys,' he said.

'Yeh.'

'Then I'm comin' with yuh.'

'It'd be no good, Abel,' said Slip. 'You know it'd be no good once you're out of your own territory. We'll hand in our badges . . . '

'It's the wrong way, Slip,' said Abel. 'The whole case oughta be handed over to the authorities.'

'Authorities,' scoffed Slip. 'What would they do? Them three killers 'ud be clear to China before the authorities got movin'. We owe these three *hombres* plenty an' we gotta get 'em ourselves . . . You know that don't yuh, Abel?'

The old man's voice was low. 'Yeh, I guess I do. It's no use me or anybody else tryin' tuh stop yuh. I guess I'd do the same myself.' He slapped his hand down suddenly on his knee. 'Tarnation! I've a good mind tuh come with yuh after all. This job's bin kinda tame lately.'

'Don't talk crazy, Abel,' said Butch gruffly. 'You're a damsight too important here. What'd the town do without yuh?'

'Get along the same as usual I guess.' The old sheriff produced a pipe and began to fill it.

The other three rolled quirlies. They were lighting up when the door swung open. They had not heard anyone approaching. They were taken by surprise. They started to their feet, hands moving downwards instinctively.

'Hold it!' said the big dark man who confronted them. He had two levelled Colts to back up his command.

The men who moved in with him had their guns drawn too. They looked as if they could use them and the sheriff and his boys had more sense than to put them to the test right now.

'Winters!' said Abel Kent.

Marshal Max Winters of El Paso kicked the door to behind him. His three men ranged themselves alongside him.

'What's the idea, marshal?' said the sheriff.

'I might ask you the same question, sheriff,' said Winters, his dark face inscrutable. 'I never expected to find the men I was after right here in your office.'

'You're makin' a mistake, marshal,' said Abel. 'These three men are my deputies.'

'I'm amazed,' said Winters mockingly. 'I didn't think you picked your deputies so haphazardly.'

'These men have been my deputies for three years.'

'Yeh? Did they tell you about the little holiday they had during which they robbed a bank an' killed a man. Then killed two other men afterwards.'

'You're barkin' up the wrong tree, marshal,' said the sheriff. 'The men you want have been here. They killed Doc

Trapps. We've just buried him. They also held up the El Paso coach. Killed the driver, the guard and another man.'

'Are you crazy . . . ? Tuh think they had the nerve. Can't yuh understand these are the men you want. These are the men I've trailed from El Paso. The bankrobbers. They killed two o' my deputies . . . '

'It's all bin a mix-up,' said Red McGrath hotly. 'But I guess it's no use tryin' to explain it all tuh you . . . ' His loud outburst had screened any sound that might have been made by the opening door. He was interrupted now by a voice that said: 'Drop those guns or I'll start blastin'.'

Time seemed to stand still, then was propelled again with a rush as guns clattered savagely on the boards.

'Get over by that wall,' said the voice. 'Then turn.'

The four men did as ordered. When Max Winters turned his look of rage was replaced by one of surprise. 'Berners!' he ejaculated. 'I never expected to find you in this neck o' the woods. What's the meanin' o' this play?'

'Hallo, Winters,' said Jack Berners, coldly. 'Still up to your little games?'

'And you,' said the marshal. 'Still stickin' your nose into other people's business.'

'Yeh . . . It's a bad habit of mine. But it often brings me joy.'

The two tall men faced each other. Winters, the darker and broader, seemed as if poised to spring. But the two guns held steadily in the other's hands held him in check. For a second naked hate flashed in both pairs of eyes. Then their faces became normal again: Berners lean, cadaverous, his expression mocking; Winters, saturnine, expressionless.

The latter said softly: 'You're bucking the law now, Berners.'

The other's lips quirked mirthlessly. 'The law!' he echoed.

Butch, Slip and Red had their guns out now. Berners turned to them.

'I guess we ain't got time to pow-wow with Mr Winters now,' he said. 'I came to see if you boys was figuring on ridin'.'

'We was,' said Butch.

'Yeh, so wuz I. I guess we think alike. My hoss's outside. I'm all ready. I shouldn't advise you to stay around here much longer either. Scarsville is full o' Mr Winters' bright boys. They're a real playful crowd I can assure yuh.'

'We'll ride,' said Butch.

'I'll get the hosses,' said Slip. He went out the back way.

A few moments later he returned. 'The hosses are out front with Berner's mount,' he said. 'The town does seem kinda crowded. I may have been spotted.'

'You ain't got a chance,' said Marshal Winters.

'We'll get movin',' said Butch. 'Abel!'

The old man shook his head. 'I've changed my mind,' he said. He hefted his guns in his hands. 'I'll have a heart-to-heart talk with the marshal as soon as you're out o' the way . . . Get movin'.'

'But, Abel, we cain't leave you here now.'

'Nuthin'll happen to me,' said Abel. He smiled. 'Me an' the marshal are old friends.'

'Abel, we . . . '

'Get movin',' said the sheriff harshly.

Butch shrugged ponderous shoulders.

'C'mon, boys . . . We'll be seein' yuh, Abel.'

'You'll be seein' me, too,' said the marshal, levelly. 'I'll remember you particularly, Jack Berners.'

'Yeh, the day will come, Max,' said Berners. He was the last to leave, running across the boardwalk, vaulting into the saddle as the others had done. The quartet galloped down the street. They lay low on their horses' backs. People gaped. Then a hard-looking stranger drew his gun, shouting.

Jack Berners fired. The man coughed,

dropped his gun, draped himself across the hitching-rail.

Red McGrath shot another man's hat off. The man dived for cover. The four horsemen left the main street and thudded along the trail in swirling dust.

# 6

## 1

Sheriff Kent puffed at his pipe with obvious enjoyment. His guns were steady, keeping the four raging men at bay. His eyes became a little bit worried as shots rang outside.

'Your pards didn't get very far,' jeered Winters.

'They're probably picking off your men as they go along,' retorted the old man . . . 'Now, now,' he chided. 'Don't strain yourself like that. You know I ain't afeard tuh shoot. Even if you all jumped at once I guess I'd get at least three o' yuh. You first, Max. It ain't worth risking is it? Don't worry; if you behave yourselves I'll put down my guns as soon as I think fit.'

'You'll suffer for this, Kent,' said Winters. His eyes blazed in his dark, taut face, his whole muscular body seemed to be surcharged with passion and tension.

There was no more shooting outside but plenty of shouting. Quite close somebody yelled, 'Marshal Winters!'

Sheriff Kent smiled again. He figured his boys had gotten away. Had gotten a good start too.

Boot heels thudded on the sidewalk outside. The sheriff lowered his guns. Winters leapt, striking savagely with balled fist. The blow took the old man full in the mouth. He went over backwards and fell behind the desk.

The door burst open. Two of the marshal's men ran in.

'Did yuh get 'em?'

'No, we didn't know what wuz happenin'. We thought . . . '

'You thought!'

Winters bent and retrieved his guns from the floor. As he straightened up with them in his hand, Sheriff Kent arose from behind the desk. Winters turned on him. For a moment the old man's life hung in the balance. He was empty-handed, his face was white, a trickle of blood stained his chin. He looked at the marshal quizzically.

'Hell, I oughta give it to yuh!' snarled Winters.

Kent smiled crookedly. 'But you won't,' he said. 'It wouldn't be wise, would it?'

Winters turned back to his men.

'Come on,' he said. 'We're wasting time.'

They trooped out. The door was slammed behind them with a force that shook the building. The sheriff's smile broadened. He slumped down in his chair and gingerly fingered his swelling lips. Someday maybe he'd get to kill the guy. Probably not. Still, it had been worth it!

Meanwhile the subjects of the sheriff's thoughts were still riding at full gallop. They had gotten a very good start and they knew the country well.

At twilight they stopped at a little settlement and bought canned foods and coffee. Then they rode on.

At nightfall they halted in a wood and built a fire. 'If Winters catches us here after the trail we've followed he's the Great White Scout himself,' said Butch.

'Nevertheless,' said Slip, 'I vote we take it in turns to stand guard.'

'First of all, chow,' said Butch and smacked his lips. 'Hand me that can o' beans, Jack.'

Berners grinned and complied. Here were three buckaroos after his own heart. It was good to be riding the trail again — even an owlhoot one.

'I never had time to say goodbye to Ann,' said Red mournfully.

'Ann?'

'Miss Ann Calthorpe,' said Red primly.

'Oh!' chorused the others.

For a while after this, all that could be heard was the slow champing of jaws. Red was the first to speak again.

He said: 'All we seem to be doin' lately is gettin' run out o' towns.'

'I've bin run outa towns by better people,' said Butch.

'I dessay you have,' said Jack Berners soberly, and he began to tell them about Marshal Max Winters. Winters had come originally from the Pecos. Perhaps that's why Abel Kent knew him so well. 'He's a damsight older than he looks,' said Berners. 'He's like an Indian. They never seem to show their age until they're really old. Then they seem to shrivel up suddenly like a nut. I've always figured he had some Indian blood in him — though both his folks were white — quite nice people, too. Maybe he's a throwback from generations. He's got all the traits of an Indian — plus plenty of intelligence — which makes things worse. He's put paid to plenty of wrong 'uns, which blinds the authorities to the fact that he's a wrong 'un himself. There's plenty like him in the West today — a marshal's badge can conceal a lot of things.'

Winters had been a deputy marshal first. The Pecos was his territory to rule

133

as he wished. His nearest superior officer was at El Paso. Winters ran his territory his own way, for his own ends. But he always managed, outwardly anyway, to keep just within the law he was supposed to represent.

'D'yuh remember Chivo Porteus?' said Berners. The three pardners confessed to having *heard* of him at least.

'They useter call him the Terror o' the Pecos,' said Red. 'What happened to him?'

'He fell from his horse and broke his neck,' said Berners with an ironic smile. 'Without him his band just dissolved . . . I figure that if Winters hadn't been a deputy marshal — and knew he was on a good thing — he'd've led 'em himself.'

'Like that, was it?'

'Yeh, he ran hand-in-glove with Chivo for years. Everybody knew it but nobody could prove it. If one of Chivo's men got out of hand it was a job for the marshal. The man was usually shot resisting arrest. Winters could always cite these cases as evidence of his zeal for duty.'

'You seem to've made a study of Winters,' said Slip.

'I have. I've had plenty of time. I've known him since he was a kid. A worse choice for a lawman would be hard to find. But I must admit he's clever. Devilishly clever. An' he knows all the people who can do him the most good. He's a purty powerful man in this neck o' the woods.' Berners voice became suddenly softer. 'But he'll get what's comin' to him one day.'

'You hate him don't yuh?' said the observant Slip bluntly.

'Hate's a funny word,' said Berners softly. 'I reckon I've got past that stage. What is to happen between me an' Winters someday is just inevitable.'

He paused. Then: 'Yuh see, he killed my young brother.'

Neither of the other three men spoke. Their faces were stern, shadowed and hollowed, then lit spasmodically by the flickering firelight.

Berners continued his soft-voiced tale as if he was telling it to himself over again. How many times had he told it over and over in his thoughts?

'Jerry wasn't a bad kid. He was just wild. He was just a store-clerk. When he wuz eighteen he got tuh figuring he oughta be somethin' better — he ought to have plenty o' money an' travel the world. He didn't understand that all a man's travellin' comes with time — that there's no short-cut to *anywhere*. He got in a fight with another clerk an' stabbed him with a paper-knife. It wasn't a bad wound. But Jerry didn't stay to find out how bad it was. He lit out for the hills an' joined up with Chivo Porteus. Chivo had been a sort of a legendary hero of his.'

Berners paused and gave a little sigh. 'Wal, I guess after a bit he discovered his mistake, an' tried to get back. About a month later Winters an' two of his men brought his body in. Winter's men testified that Jerry went for his gun first an' the marshal had to shoot him. Jerry wasn't a gunman. He was just a clerk. Winters was the fastest-drawin' man in the territory — the kid never had a chance. Of course I accused Winters. I picked a fight with him.' Berners shrugged. 'I got run out of the territory by his men and was told I'd be shot on sight if I showed my face there again . . . I got a job with the railroad. A bit later I heard that Winters had been made marshal of El Paso.'

The voice died away in the silence. Butch leaned forward and put a small log gently on the fire.

Berners rose to his feet. 'You three get some shut-eye,' he said. 'I'll take the first lookout.' He turned and made his way slowly out of the circle of firelight.

2

The town of Sarido consisted of one main street which was almost a mile long. It was flanked on both sides by buildings of every shape and description: corrugated sheeting, logs, wood-frame, adobe, but not one brick-built one among them.

The street climbed upwards to the slopes of the hills behind. Four cabins, one of them a general store, at the bottom of the street, were in US territory. Then came the stream, which only ran in autumn, crossing the street. When a man stepped across that stream and began to climb he was in Mexico. If he continued to climb and left the street behind pretty soon he found himself among the craggy wastes of that lawless country. There was very little there except a few wild animals to whom man was a queer creature from another world. Nevertheless, some men, for reasons best known to themselves continued to climb. That's not counting crazy prospectors who'll climb anything in search of that dull metal of which very few of them ever discover a worthwhile amount.

But to return to Sarido. This town's

main product, its only justification for existence in that wild land, was vice, and, in particular, gambling. It was the rendezvous and hidey-hole of people who loved to take a chance — or had already taken one, and were fleeing from its consequences. The Mexican *Federales* were too busy chasing bandits to bother much about Sarido. Every now and then they swooped down on it to pick up a miscreant of their own race, but usually they left the American people of the town severely alone.

The number of Sarido's regular population was little more than five dozen, above half of them ladies (of a kind). The rest fluctuated greatly; some people stayed little more than a night before moving on. From time to time bunches of Texas lawmen arrived, only to return to their own provinces with disgruntled expressions on their lean hard features.

Jim Corey, Eastern gunman and big-shot gambler, was uncrowned king of Sarido. He was owner of most of the nine casinos, if those ramshackle honky-tonks and liquor shops could be labelled such. Most of the girls worked for him and also a bunch of thugs, whose job it was to keep the peace — which meant that if any luckless waddy raised a squeal about being cheated he must be shut-up — and pronto! Some of the things that happened in Sarido would not have been tolerated even in Texas. But this was Mexico, and as long as the rash did not spread too far who was to care. If a few gringoes shot each other to pieces every now and then what business was it of the *Federales*. A few less gringoes, that was all. But a Mexican lawbreaker was not encouraged to seek sanctuary in Sarido. He was yanked out of it pretty damn' quick. And, needless to say, in cases like this Jim Corey proved to be very cooperative with the authorities. For a glorious night or two Mexican law was the guest of honour in Sarido. Then the doomed captive was dragged away to be host at the very brink of his own unmarked grave. From every point of view except his it was a pretty satisfactory arrangement all round.

One afternoon among the new arrivals in town were three men. One was fat and wore spectacles, another was red-headed and mean-looking, and the third was small and lean and had teeth like a lobo. They gambled a little and interfered with nobody. They slept the night there, then on the following morning rode quite sedately up into the hills.

It was another week or so before Sarido saw them again. Then one night they rode in and hitched their horses outside Corey's Palace, which was the town's main saloon and casino, probably due to the fact that it was the only one with a garishly-painted false front — which, although the building was only two storeys high, made it look at least three.

The three men entered the Palace

and got their liquor. Then the fat man and the little lean one joined in a poker-game while the redhead wandered off on his own and got attached to a roulette-wheel.

It was getting late; gaming, drinking and everything else, was in full swing. The place was packed. Many of the people were strangers to each other. Many had never been in the place before. Nobody took any notice of three more strangers in the mêlée.

When a player wanted chips to gamble with he bought them from a hard-faced *hombre* who sat behind a little iron grill beside the bar. If he wanted his chips cashed he saw the same man. The hard-faced man was custodian of a heap of money. But it was cheek-by-jowl with a sawn-off gun loaded with buckshot, and two Colts.

It was close on midnight when the redhead got himself hitched-up with a luscious half-breed girl and forsook the roulette-wheel for a comparatively quiet spot at a table which was, incidentally, quite close to the little cage which housed the hard-faced *hombre*. The latter did not give the amorous couple a second glance. And pretty soon his attention was drawn by something that was happening in another quarter of the room.

At the poker-table the redhead's snaggle-toothed runt of a pardner had thrown down his cards in disgust, kicked back his chair and slouched away to the bar. A few seconds later the fat man was also cursing and accusing the other players of being a lot of dirty sharpers. His huge arms turned the table up, and chairs and men with it.

At the bar the runt drew two guns and with a rapid and deadly burst of shooting put out the lights. In the sudden pitch darkness a woman's scream cut above all the babble. Then gunshots boomed again and a male voice answered in agony.

There was panic as everybody tried to find the door at once. It was a full seven minutes before someone lit a hurricane lantern and bathed the scene in flickering light.

The place was half-empty now, but as the light streamed into the street those outside began to trickle in again.

Behind the bar stood plump, florid Jim Corey. His face was black as the night. At his feet lay a dead bartender, at his side the hard-faced man in the cage had his head laid sideways on his little counter. A bullet had entered his left ear and spattered his brains among the coloured chips and the small change. The bag that held his takings, in tightly-rolled or crumpled bills, had disappeared . . .

It hung now on the pommel of a saddle on the back of a black horse ridden by the mean-looking redhead as, with his two pards, he wended his way through the foothills in the direction of the Sierra Madre.

He was jubilant at the success of his scheme and at the deadliness of his own shooting.

'Right through the side o' the haid,'

he chuckled. 'An' in the dark too. I had to slug the girl though before I could get a line on him.'

Lafe the runt broke in at this juncture. 'So I suppose it's nothin' tuh shoot out a pair of lights then turn around an' shoot the bartender . . . '

'Yeh, that was fine work, Lafe,' said Ginger off-handedly.

'Ef'n you two'll quit patting yourselves on the back for a bit spare a thought for me,' said fat Monty, peevishly. 'I was liable to be at the receivin' end of a gun instead of the other one. Next time maybe one o' you'll start the ruckus.'

'Aw, quit moanin',' said Ginger.

'Anyway,' said Lafe, 'you ain't fast enough to do either o' the other jobs. You'd finish up by gettin' us all shot.'

'Yeh, you oughta start slimmin',' said Ginger nastily. 'An' besides you know you can't see straight since you started wearin' them spectacles.'

'It was your idea wasn't it?' growled

the fat man and lapsed into injured silence.

Ginger continued to pat himself on the back.

'This suttinly is some layout,' he said. 'We kin lose Corey's mob easily in these hills. I guess we know all the hidey-holes by now. An' I guess it'll be a long time before the *Federales* start chasin' Americans. What difference does it make tuh them how much we raid Sarido . . . '

'Later we kin start crossin' the border and doin' a few banks an' sech,' said Lafe. 'An' hop back here an' . . . '

'Yeh, yeh, I wuz comin' tuh that,' Ginger's tone was resentful, nasty.

Lafe shut up but, cloaked by the darkness, his face wore an ugly look.

3

Jack Berners reined-in his horse on the crest of the rise.

'Down ahead lies Sarido,' he said.

'Then the ground climbs again into Mexico. Real bandit country up there. I guess that's where we'll find our men.'

Twilight was a short interval between torrid day and black night with its chilly mists. Lights winked on in Sarido as the three men watched.

'Now the place's jest comin' alive,' said Berners.

'Wal, I guess night's the best time tuh ride in,' said Slip. 'We wouldn't attract much attention. It'll be purty late when we get there won't it?'

'Yeh, there's quite a piece to go yet. An' in Sarido strangers seldom attract any attention at all. It's a town of strangers — outlaws most of 'em . . . Altho',' added Berners, 'maybe I'd better ride in alone first an' scout around. Anyway, if those three killers do happen to be there I guess they wouldn't recognize me, whereas they're sure to spot you three.'

'You got a point there, Jack,' said Butch.

'Yeh, I guess we had better hang

behind while you go an' scout,' said Slip. 'An' if you do see them three jaspers, Jack, come a-runnin'.'

'I'll come right back anyway,' said the tall man. 'Gimme half-an-hour or so.'

The lights of Sarido were much nearer now. The four men reached a small grove of trees.

'I guess this is as good a place as any to bivouac,' said Red.

'Yeh, we kin light a fire. I'm hungry.' This from Butch. Slip had lapsed into silence once more. He did not break it. He just slid from his horse.

'I'll ride on then, boys,' said Jack Berners. 'Be seein' yuh.'

'So-long.'

Berners rode direct to town and straight into the main street. It was autumn and the thin shallow stream that was the borderline between America and Mexico showed a thin trickle, a wriggling silver thread in the darkness. The tall man's horse approached it cautiously as if it were a new species of rattlesnake then stepped over it gingerly.

Berners eased his mount gently up the now-sloping street. He looked around at the bright lights, the men and women bound for a night of pleasure. Sarido hadn't changed much. It looked maybe a little more prosperous. The tall man dismounted outside Corey's Palace. He hitched his horse to the rail. His steps were purposeful, his boot heels thudded on the boardwalk. He swung open the double doors and strode into the smoke, the people and the noise.

His boldness went unnoticed. He was just another stranger among hundreds of them. An outlaw; a killer maybe. Who cared? No, Sarido had not changed at all.

The tall man breasted the bar and ordered a long one. He turned and surveyed the occupants of the large room, surveyed them in a disinterested manner, warily and without impertinence. If he recognized anyone the fact was not revealed by any flicker of emotion in his expressionless face.

He turned back to the bar, took his drink and paid for it. On the other side of the bar, a few yards away from the barman, a man was standing looking at him. Their eyes met.

'Hello, Jim,' said Berners.

'Hello, Jack.' The other man stepped forward. They shook hands.

Jim Corey hadn't changed much. He was a little plumper and his face was pink with good living. He looked prosperous and contented. There was no hint of grey in his thick, straight black hair.

He said: 'Long time no see.'

'Yeh, how've yuh bin?'

Corey shrugged. 'Can't grumble. I've kept out of trouble.'

Berners smiled thinly. 'Trust you for that.'

The two men eyed each other warily. Then both of them smiled.

'Still workin' for the railroad, Jack?' said Corey.

'Yeh.'

'Here in your official capacity?'

'Nope, not this time, Jim.'

Corey called the bartender. 'Have this one on the house, Jack.'

'Thanks.'

They took their drinks. The bartender moved away again. Corey leaned closer to the tall railwayman.

'What brings yuh here, Jack? Trouble?'

'Nothin' very tragic,' said Berners with studied nonchalance. He did not intend to tell Jim Corey anything yet. Later maybe he might be of help. Then again he might not. You never could tell with Jim. In a way Berners admired the man. He thought the admiration was mutual between them. But it was a guarded admiration — they owed each other nothing. Any day it might be each man for himself. And Jim Corey was a bad enemy. To incur his enmity in this territory was little short of suicide.

To forestall any more questioning on the part of Corey, Berners asked one himself.

'Anythin' happened around town lately?'

'The faro bank was held up last night,' said Corey laconically. 'They got away with a cool three thousand or so. Three men.'

Berners gave an inward start, but he was too old a campaigner to reveal his overpowering interest by word or manner.

He evinced a tepid regard. 'Three men,' he echoed. 'Greasers?'

'No, three Americans. I didn't see much of 'em myself but I got their descriptions, a bit varied and garbled. I gathered there was a big man wearing spectacles, a red-haired man and a skinny little runt.' Corey gave Berners an enquiring glance. The latter did not speak.

Corey continued; 'They killed one o' the barmen and Bruiser Phil, the checker . . . '

Berners was impressed. 'They must've been fast to get the drop on Phil.'

'The hold-up was well thought out,'

said Corey sardonically. 'I couldn't've done it better myself.' He explained to Berners how it had been done and the latter was moved to say, 'You've certainly got to hand it to 'em whoever they were.'

It seemed to him that Corey looked at him very keenly. Had something in his manner betrayed the fact that he knew these three men? It was queer that Corey had not asked that very question. He knew he mustn't keep silent too long or the saloon-owner would be really suspicious. He pretended to be pondering over the stick-up men's ingenuity, a little smile on his lips. But he must say something soon . . . He was saved from doing so by the sudden arrival of a bartender who told the boss he was wanted out back.

Corey rose. 'Excuse me, Jack,' he said. He followed the barman.

Berners sipped his drink reflectively. He took a long time over it and he was thinking all the time. He emptied his glass and took it to the bar to be replenished. Then he returned to the table. He must learn more about these three men and their latest escapade. He awaited Corey's return.

But time passed and the saloon-owner did not come back. Berners knew he must go or the boys would be worrying about him. They might even come after him. After what he had just heard he could not risk that. Although plenty of folks had seen the three killers it seemed they hadn't had a chance to get a real good impression of them. Berners decided to ride back pronto and tell the boys what he had already learned. He went to the bar and told the bartender that when Mr Corey returned to tell him that his friend had had to go but would be back later. Pretty soon he was galloping down the outward trail once more.

The night was very dark. The few stars, very high, like twinkling pin-points in the dark void above gave very little light. But Berner's horse was sure-footed, thudding purposefully along the trail. The trail was lonesome, a little keen wind soughed. Berners looked forward to the camp-fire he knew the boys had lit. Not far to go now. He had news too. The boys would be glad of it . . .

Suddenly Berners stiffened in the saddle. Behind the thudding tremor of the hooves of his own mount he thought he heard others. He slowed down to a gentle trot. The riders were in front of him, just jogging along. Probably just a bunch of cowpokes heading into town. Nevertheless, Berners went cautiously.

The sounds came nearer, much nearer, then two horsemen loomed out of the darkness.

'Jack,' yelled a voice.

The two men reined in. It was Red and Slip. Despite himself Berners was mightily relieved. It would not be pleasant to meet strange men on this trail. People bound for Sarido were often jumpy and liable to shoot before asking questions.

'Hello, boys,' he said cheerily. 'Did you think I'd got lost?'

'No,' replied Red. 'But we think Butch has.'

'Butch? I thought maybe you'd come out tuh meet me an' left Butch behind in the grove.'

'No, we're lookin' for him. That brown stallion o' his that he's so fond of wandered off an' he went to look for it. He wuz out so long we thought mebbe he'd tripped in a gopher-hole or su'thin' an' sprained his ankle so we went out a-lookin, We found the stallion, he's tied up now back among the trees, but we can't see hide nor hair o' Butch. You ain't seen him have yuh?'

'Nope.'

'Wal,' said Slip. 'He can't get far on foot that's certain-sure. Not in them ridin' boots o' his. Butch's got more savvy than to get lost. I figure he must've met with a accident or somethin'. The only thing we can do is keep lookin'.'

'If he's got back to camp he'll probably be wondering where you are right now,' said Berners.

'Yeh, there's that,' said Red. 'I guess we'd better ride back there first, hadn't we?'

# 7

## 1

When Butch left the grove he walked a
few yards in the darkness, then halted
and stood listening. The wind soughed
and, every now and then, gave a little
blustery gust. It irritated Butch and he
cursed. Then he pursed his lips and
whistled. Then listened again.

Far below him in the valley glittered
the lights of Sarido. The stars above,
very high, were like distant reflections
of these lights. They gave very little
illumination as Butch peered into the
darkness, cursed the wind, then
whistled again. Still whistling he began
to walk forward.

He paused again, suddenly. Was that
hoof-beats he heard or just a trick
played by the wind? Far away somewhere, like a thin echo from another

158

sphere, a coyote howled.

But Butch's surmise had been correct. The sounds he heard were hoof-beats. And coming nearer. The big man listened a bit more then turned at right angles and began to walk again. For a moment the sounds were muffled by the blustering of the wind. As it died down again the sounds became much clearer. Butch stopped in his tracks. It seemed to him there was more than one horse. Or was that just another trick of the pesky wind? He stayed still, his hand on his gun.

The hoof-beats thudded nearer and nearer until they seemed to be sounding almost from the depths of the ground beneath his feet. Two horsemen loomed up in the darkness, so close to him that they almost ran him down. They reined in their mounts.

'Kinda late tuh be wandering around on foot,' said one, leaning forward in his saddle and peering at Butch. The other one merely grunted.

Butch said: 'I lost my horse.'

'Headin' for Sarido?'

'Is that Sarido down below?' said Butch innocently.

'It is.'

'Wal, I guess its as good a place as any tuh ride to.' Butch was watching the man who leaned forward and talked to him. The other seemed disinterested in the whole proceedings.

But he came alive suddenly, drawing his gun, taking Butch by surprise.

'It's the big feller with glasses,' he said harshly. 'Take your hand away from that gun, *hombre*. Elevate — both of 'em!'

Standing as he was, right in the path of the two horses and their riders, Butch was at a decided disadvantage. He dare not risk a break.

He raised his hands. 'I ain't argufying with that Colt you got up there, stranger,' he drawled. 'But I'd like to know what your game is. If this is a stick-up you'll get very poor pickings.'

'He'd like tuh know what our game is,' jeered the man with the gun.

The other one leaned closer across his horse's neck. 'I guess you hit the bull this time, Dink,' he said. 'The boss will be pleased.'

'Rope him, Jugger,' said the gunman harshly.

Jugger reached for his riata. He raised it, making a loop. For a split-second the other's attention was diverted. Butch went for his gun.

Even as he got it from its holster the loop snaked over his shoulders and was pulled taut pinning his arms to his sides. His gun was clenched in his hand but he could not do a thing with it. If he pressed the trigger he was liable to shoot his own toes off.

The two men laughed. 'Drop it,' said the man with the rope.

Without a word Butch dropped it.

Jugger jerked the rope viciously.

'C'mon, big boy,' he said. 'Let's get moving.'

He turned his horse suddenly and Butch was almost pulled from his feet.

'I don't know what your game is,' he

said. 'But by . . . ' He broke off with a strangled curse as the horse started forward, pulling him to his knees. The two men laughed.

'You'll hafta be quicker'n that, big boy,' said Jugger. 'Let's see yuh run, yuh skunk, it'll get yuh in trim for when you're kicking on the end of that other rope we've already got fixed-up for yuh back in town.'

The phlegmatic Butch lost his temper suddenly and dived for Jugger's legs. He caught hold of one of them and tugged, trying to bring his man down. So sudden was his attack that Jugger was taken by surprise and was almost unseated. His pard, Dink, spurred his horse forward, released his one foot from the stirrup and kicked Butch viciously in the side of the head.

The big man fell heavily. Jugger cursed. 'Watch him, Dink,' he said. 'He's like a damned grizzly — an' just as treacherous.'

Butch rose to his knees. He certainly looked like a grizzly bear as he grunted and shook his head violently. He rose slowly. He seemed dazed. But Jugger was not taking any chances. He jerked the rope, backing his horse until the line was taut and the big man staggered forward at the end of it. He looked up at his captors, vague menacing shapes in the gloom.

Dink had drawn his gun again, it glinted dully in his hand. He said harshly: 'Don't try any more tricks, big feller, or I'll suttinly plug yuh.'

'Move,' barked Jugger. He started his horse off. Butch was compelled to trot along at the end of the rope. He did not curse or speak again, he saved his breath. But in his soul was black murder. He had guessed by now for whom the two men had mistaken him: evidently the three killers had already been up to their tricks in this district. Here was another score to be chalked up against them, as well as against the two laughing jackasses up above there.

They approached Sarido without using the actual trail.

Dink said: 'We'd better go in the back way.'

Jugger had tied his end of the riata to the pommel of his saddle. The line was taut, Butch was only just managing to keep up the pace. Although he carried a lot of weight he was hard and fit; what choked him up and shortened his breath now was hot, seething hate. He'd get those two if it was the last thing he did. He'd like to tear them to pieces with his bare hands. He flexed his cold, cramped fingers as if he already had his hands on his tormentors. These muscular movements, small though they were, caused him agony, so tight was the rope around his arms. The side of his face was sore and felt wet where Dink had kicked him.

The two horsemen began to make a detour. The lights of the town appeared one by one as they approached the dark gloomy backs of the buildings, where only a glimmer showed here and there. Finally they halted at the rear of a two-storey frame building, no more

164

prepossessing and in fact, little different to its neighbours.

The two men dismounted. As Jugger untied the rope from his saddle Dink went closer to their captive and levelled the gun at him.

'Watch yerself, big feller,' he warned. 'Walk in front o' me. Foller where Jugger pulls.' He finished the sentence with a little snigger.

Butch had difficulty in restraining himself from diving at him. But he was not quite foolhardy enough to throw his life away in that manner.

Jugger tugged at the rope and without a word Butch followed him across the hard uneven ground and through a door on to a creaking board floor.

They moved along a passage illuminated only by the diffused light coming from the half-open door at the end of it. Jugger flung the door open wide and pulled Butch into the room after him. Dink followed, his gun held ready. He kicked the door to behind him with the heel of his boot.

They were in a small but very luxuriously-appointed office. A mahogany table-desk, a well-padded horseshoe swivel-chair. A wine-red thick pile carpet into which the heavy dusty boots of the men sank like a desecration. Against the wall to the right of them was a large safe, its heavy black steel doors shining in the lamplight. To the left was a small but very comfortable-looking couch and an intricately-carved cabinet which looked like an antique. Far from antique were the two bottles of liquor which stood atop of it, the three empty glasses and the box of best cheroots.

Jugger looped another coil of rope deftly around Butch and pulled it tight.

'Watch him, Dink,' he said. 'I'll go get the boss.'

'I'll watch him,' said the other. 'I'll blow his haid off if he tries anythin' funny.'

Revealed in the light, Dink was lean, pale and cadaverous. Jugger, lithe, medium, but very ugly (his nickname suited him) swiftly left the room.

'Mind if I sit down?' said Butch.

Dink grunted. He jerked the gun. 'All right,' he said. 'But watch yourself.'

'Cain't do much trussed up like a turkey-cock,' said Butch blandly.

Dink eyed him suspiciously. The small couch groaned protestingly as the big man plumped down on it. His spectacles glinted in the lamplight. His tough craggy face was composed, swollen on one side where Jugger's boot had connected. A jagged line of dried blood ran from the swelling down to the jawbone. An inanimate docile hulk though he was now, Butch still looked very dangerous. Those huge hands that were pinned to his side looked capable of quite easily crushing the life from the slender Dink. The cadaverous man thanked his saints for the tight rope, and kept his gun steadily levelled at the captive.

Bootheels thudded in the passage outside The door swung open once more and and a well set-up, plump, dark man entered. His black hair was sleek. His dark eyes were like polished marbles, expressionless as he looked at the prisoner.

Jim Corey had lived by his wits nearly all his life and had schooled himself not to show emotion under any circumstances. Inwardly he was jubilant at his boys' success on picking up the bespectacled hold-up man. Apart from the loss of the money there was the murder of Bruiser Phil to be considered. Phil had been with Corey a good many years and the implacable king of Sarido had been as attached to him as much as his cold nature would allow him to be attached to anyone.

Smirking, very proud of himself, the unprepossessing Jugger followed Corey ino the room.

'That's him I declare, boss,' he said.

'He certainly bears out the description,' said Corey, then addressing Butch directly, his dark eyes dispassionately questioning. 'What've you got to say for yourself, big feller?'

'That goes for you too,' said Butch,

his voice very deep with passion. 'Are you the king-pin around here?'

'I am.'

'What's your game then? If it's robbery, like I told your two boys here, you've come unstuck this time.'

Corey grinned, showing white even teeth. 'Actin' the innocent, hey?' he said.

'Innocent? What yuh getting at? What's your idea?' burst out Butch. In an excess of passion he lunged forward. He was brought to an impotent standstill by the tightening coils of the rope.

'Evidently he ain't in no mood to talk now,' said Corey. 'We'll see what a night in the cellar'll do to him. Take him down.'

Holding the end of the rope, Dink walked round in front of his captive. 'C'mon,' he said and jerked.

Corey and his jug-faced side-kick, who still held his gun ready, stepped to one side. As Butch, in the wake of Dink passed the former he hissed: 'I'll make yuh jump for this, yuh panty-waisted bastard.'

The saloon-owner's features darkened, his lips writhed. He seemed as if he would strike the big man. But he checked himself and only smiled thinly, the polished gentleman once more.

'Go with them Jugger,' he said.

Dink led Butch down a narrow dark passage which ran at right-angles to the one along which they walked when they entered the building. At the end of the narrow murky cleft was a wooden door which Dink opened.

'Come on,' he said, jerking the rope. He stepped aside, drawing his gun as he did so. There was not much room in the little passage and the prisoner was big and irritatingly awkward. He lurched and, with his heavy, trussed body, managed to jolt the skinny man against the wall with not inconsiderable violence. Dink cursed, he had a job to hold on to his gun. With Butch's weight against him he could not do anything with it. It dangled in his hand.

Jugger came nearer. Butch kicked Dink on the shins. The thin man yelped. Jugger cursed and swung his gun. Butch pivoted, all his clumsiness leaving him. He caught the blow on his shoulder. If only he had his hands free!

There wasn't enough room to dodge the next swipe. The barrel of the Colt slammed against his neck. He staggered, feeling sudden, sickening pain. The ground opened in a black, yawning gap beneath his feet. He tumbled down a short flight of slippery steps. Instinctively he let his body go limp as he hit hard ground. He hadn't been an expert bulldozer for nothing. As he tried to collect his senses he heard the voice of Jugger say 'So-long, big boy.' Then the door slammed and he was in pitch-blackness.

## 2

He lay supine for a few moments feeling the darkness like a velvety cloak

171

around him. A cloak that for a time billowed and almost choked him with sudden vertigo. This passed and he felt suddenly helpless, frustrated; the inevitable reactions of a being, bred and living in the great outdoors, suddenly enclosed and trapped. The darkness was impenetrable. He tried to rise, then cursed, realizing his hands were bound, the thongs cutting cruelly into his thick, muscular wrists.

He lay again, letting the helpless choler subside, feeling the strength slowly replace it. Then methodically, a sudden grin cracking his bruised face, he squirmed up on to his knees. He rested on his haunches, all his senses keen and alert now. He became suddenly aware of an odour almost as thick as the darkness around him. He was surprised that he had not sensed it before. It was the odour of raw whiskey.

He grinned again and took a good deep sniff. He could do with a glass of the raw, pungent stuff right now. But a sniff was better than nothing. He braced himself, then lurched upwards on to his feet. But they failed to find a grip on the slimy uneven floor. He teetered, then fell heavily. He swore loudly, but without much violence. Now his temper had subsided it would take more than a couple of tumbles to daunt him. He squirmed laboriously to his knees again. If only Slip Anderson could see him now — wouldn't the lean, runny have some cause to jeer at his pardner's weight. Butch grinned again then winced as a spasm of pain shot through the bruised flesh of his face. He felt no sudden hot malice against Dink and Jugger now. Only a cold certainty that ultimately they would pay for their cavalier treatment of their erstwhile prisoner.

Suddenly he realized what a mug he was, lurching about in the middle of the cellar like this. If he got up against the wall . . . He began to lollop along on his knees. It was an awkward and night-mare progress, forging ahead recklessly into the pitch blackness and whatever pitfalls it might contain. He did not have far to go to meet his first obstacle. He led with his jutting chin to something hard and smooth which rocked him back on his haunches and made the blackness suddenly full of white flashes. He waited until his head had stopped spinning, then wagged it from side to side experimentally.

Then he inclined it gently until his temple rested on the smooth cool surface before him. The odour of whiskey was much stronger now. Butch lowered his head. His forehead touched cold steel. Then he knew his surmize was correct. The object he leaned against was a barrel of hooch.

He got to his feet quite easily and learnt that there was another barrel atop this one. And another couple beside it. And another couple the other side. The place was stacked out with them. He was obviously in the cellar of a saloon — probably the *only* cellar in such a shantytown as Sarido.

He turned around and began to feel

along the barrels with his fingers. Something bit deeply into his thumb. He swore. But the pain was welcome. It proved that he had found what he sought; a jagged edge on a steel hoop that encircled one of the barrels. His captors certainly had not done much figuring. Just tossed him down here like so much garbage. Probably expecting him to lie and twiddle his thumbs. He grinned wolfishly in the darkness and set to work.

He stopped grinning suddenly. Breath hissed from between clenched teeth as his hands slipped and the jagged steel lacerated his wrist. But the thongs became looser. That last painful jerk had almost severed them. Butch manoeuvred a bit more and sawed away.

The bands parted entirely and Butch felt the scalding agony of returning circulation. He brought his hands to the front of him. The movements gave him more pain. He raised his left hand to his mouth and began to suck his torn and bleeding wrist. The blood was salty;

it tasted good. Now he was ready for anything or anybody. No matter how many of them. He began to feel in his vest pocket for matches then realized that Jugger had frisked him.

He began to feel his way along the barrels. Again he found what he sought. A bung: just slightly protruding. He caught hold of it with one huge hand and pulled. It was a tough one but could not withstand his Herculean strength for long. He grunted as it came out with the dull plop and whiskey gushed coldly over his hand. He let it slop on his wounded wrist, biting into the lacerated flesh until he could have howled with the pain of it. He dabbed it gently on his face. It stung but it felt good. He cupped his hands beneath the stream then raised them to his lips. It was real rotgut. For a moment it almost took his breath away. If Slip and Red could only see him now.

He drank what he needed — he knew his capacity — then replaced the bung, stilling the gurgling tide. He began to walk slowly across the cellar in the direction he judged the steps to be. He stubbed his toe against the wall and only saved his face from further punishment by a swiftly raised hand. He turned, steering himself with his right hand against the wall. He felt his way cautiously along. He came once more up against barrels — smaller kegs this time by the feel of 'em. There was certainly plenty of stock down here. Enough for ages of rip-snorting nights . . .

He turned again, then stiffened. The sound of footsteps came from up above, came nearer . . .

Light streamed down the cellar-steps as the door above opened. A lantern shone, illuminating the cadaverous features of the spindly Dink as he gingerly descended the steps. The light gleamed dully on the barrel of the gun held in the hand of Jugger, advancing behind him. Both of them peered, their heads turning. Something swished curiously in a corner . . .

Dink never knew what hit him. It was a keg, slung with terrific force, breaking his skull as if it were a rotten coconut. The lamp crashed to the floor, Dink on top of it. There was a shower of sparks then utter blackness. Then the cellar became illuminated briefly again as Jugger began blazing away.

The silence was absolute once more. Jugger waited and listened. He began to work his way slowly backwards up the cellar steps. Again something swished. A keg crashed at Jugger's feet right on the place he had occupied a second before. The ugly man cursed vilely and fired again twice. In the flashes he saw the big figure looming over him and he knew he had missed. Something that felt like a lump of rock hit him in the temple. His gun was wrenched from his grasp and he was flung down the cellar steps like a rag doll, to join his dead partner at the bottom.

When Butch reached the passage two men were running towards him. They were taken by surprise and both dead from a few well-placed shots before they could do anything about it. Butch threw away the empty gun, scooped up two loaded ones from their disinterested owners, and charged onwards. Neither of the two men was the dark, sleek-faired skunk whom he sought.

He ploughed on along to the door of the office. He flung it open. Darkness greeted him. Before him, silence. Behind him, shouting voices, getting nearer. Then Butch's eyes lit up behind his spectacles as, turning he saw the man he sought. In the same instant he fired from the hip . . .

Jim Corey cried out with pain as his gun was spun forcibly away from his scorched hand. Then, even as his men from the bar room behind, reached him, the big feller did too. Corey ducked as Butch grabbed.

The others were scared to shoot because of their boss. One of them swung at the big feller with a gun-barrel. He missed. His muscle was gripped by a bunch of fingers that felt like a steel clamp. Another hand grabbed the front of his shirt and he was tossed along the passage. His head hit the wall with a crack and he lost all interest in the subsequent proceedings.

In the passage there was no more room than for three men abreast and even then they got in each other's way. Corey did not lack guts. He rose, grappling Butch around the waist. The big man hit him once across the neck with one of the guns. He went down. That'd keep him quiet till he was wanted, reflected Butch grimly. Then, before the others could start throwing lead across the prostrate body of their boss the big man began blasting.

The two big Colts echoed and re-echoed bloody murder in the confined space. Acrid smoke, the stink of cordite, screaming lead, the agonized cries of dying or wounded men . . .

As Corey groaned and raised his head, four of his men fell around him. Another leaned against the passage wall, coughing blood.

A huge hand grabbed the saloon owner by his collar and hauled him to his feet. With the dazed man propelled before him Butch forged on, making for the nearest door which was half open. If he heard the babble of noise that came from beyond it, it did not seem to worry him none. He only stopped to collect another gun from the floor to replace his empty one. Then he pushed Corey roughly before him, using him as a means to swing the door open wide.

They were in the bar-room, behind the bar. A white aproned man swung up a shotgun, wide-eyed. Butch fired once. The man dropped the gun and clutched at his paunch. He screamed, his eyes rolling now. Then he crumpled to the floor and began to writhe, still scream-ing. The saloon was pretty full, but people were leaving. Things didn't seem none too healthy. Those that remained would never forget the big man with the steel-rimmed spectacles still clipped securely to his rather bulbous nose, his battered face grim and awesome.

Butch pushed Corey before him through the trap in the bar. His one gun was prodded into the saloon-owner's back, the other menaced the crowd.

There was dead silence except for the soft, gurgling whimpering of the wounded man behind the bar. Then the big man spoke.

'If anybody tries to stop me the boss here gets it plumb in the spine. An' I'm purty sure to get a few more besides him. I shouldn't none of you risk anythin' if I wuz you.'

The crowd had receded. Butch forced his prisoner across the cleared space.

Corey had pretty well regained his senses by now. 'You'll pay for this,' he hissed.

Butch shouted: 'Open up there.' Then, quieter, in Corey's ear, 'You'd better tell 'em to open up.'

'Better open up, folks,' said Corey. He knew when he was licked.

Boot-heels scraped as the crowd parted to let the two men through.

Then there was silence again. The man behind the bar was silent now, too.

Butch and his captive passed through the ranks. The former with a sideways motion, trying to protect his flank as well.

A man stepped into the cleared space behind them. A gun glinted in his fist. He fired at the same time as Butch.

The big man staggered a little as agonizing fire seared his side. He fired again. But the man was already crumpling. The crowd shifted.

'Any more?' yelled Butch, hoarsely, 'Back! Back!' His eyes gleamed wildly behind his spectacles. 'Back I tell yuh! Before I start spraying lead around.'

Those nearest looked nervous and began to back. Butch said in Corey's ear. 'Keep movin! Faster! Quick, before I put a slug in yuh.' His voice was savage and intense. Corey quickened his pace.

They reached the batwings. Corey went through them. As Butch followed he suddenly thumbed the hammer of his gun and sent a couple of shots just above the heads of the crowd. One daring gent retaliated wildly but only smashed a window. The crowd scattered.

There were plenty horses at the hitching-rack outside. Butch selected the two nearest.

'Git up,' he said harshly.

Silently, Corey obeyed. He wasn't arguing with this madman. Butch mounted with surprising agility for a man of his bulk. If his wound gave him a twinge he did not show it.

A face appeared at the lighted window of the saloon. Butch fired. Glass tinkled and the face vanished.

'Git movin',' said Butch.

Corey urged his horse forward. Butch steered his mount up alongside him, keeping the saloon-owner between him and the saloon.

'Faster,' he growled.

They set their horses at a gallop.

Behind them shots sounded but nothing came near. Probably the folks back there were just letting off steam. They wouldn't risk potting King Corey. Pretty soon, however, hooves began to clatter raggedly as horses were pulled away from the hitching-rack.

3

Now that his passion had subsided Butch felt suddenly tired. The wound in his side, though he figured it was only a flesh one, was beginning to play him up. He could feel the warm blood trickling down his leg. He forced himself to sit upright. He kept his horse a little behind Corey's mount. His gun, steady in his hand, was pointed at the man's side. And Butch meant to shoot if the bare-headed, black-haired gink tried to make a break.

Keeping his perch in the saddle by a tight pressure of his knees to the horse's flanks, Butch let go of the reins and gingerly pressed his hand to his side. It was warmly, stickily wet when he drew it away. He was losing blood steadily.

Corey turned his head. Butch grabbed the reins again, elevated a little the gun in his other hand.

'Keep goin', pardner,' he said. 'Don't get any funny ideas.'

'You're wounded ain't yuh?' said Corey conversationally.

'It won't help you if I am,' said Butch harshly. He had a sudden impulse to press the trigger and end it right there and then. But he knew he wouldn't. The saloon-man had guts: Butch could not shoot him down like a cur. They were out on the trail now, Butch held his head high, letting the wind blow into his face.

'Faster,' he snarled at Corey. 'You're slowing down. Don't be tricky. Set her goin' before I nick yuh to liven yuh up a bit.'

Corey did not answer but kicked his heels into his mount. They galloped all out, the wind whipping at them. To Butch it was a nightmare ride of shooting, sickening pain. The gun felt like a chunk of lead in his hand. He hoped he could hold out till they got to the grove where he hoped to find Slip, Red and Jack.

'Turn off the trail here,' he yelled at Corey.

The saloon-owner obeyed. He was forcing his horse to the utmost. Maybe he thought he could make a break that way. Or perhaps he figured the rough riding would make the wounded man pass out.

Butch forced his mount after him. The grass slashed their horses' legs, the wind whipped and blustered past them.

Suddenly the big man shouted. 'Hold it! Hold it! Draw him in.' Then, as Corey did not comply with the demand. 'D'yuh hear me? Hold it, or by God I'll let yuh have it in the back.'

Corey heard him all right. He stopped taking chances and reined in his mount. He, too had heard the sound of hooves in the distance. He had hoped it was his own men coming up. But now he realized the sound was in front instead of behind. Still maybe it was better for him that way. He wouldn't trust the big feller's trigger finger if his own men did catch up. A dead King Corey wouldn't be any use to anybody.

Butch drew his gun in, held it close to him, so that it was hidden by the saddle.

'Just canter along. If these people come up, act as if we're jest goin' fer a friendly little ride. Remember I've still got the gun on yuh. The least leetle thing is liable to cause me tuh start blastin'.'

'I ain't aimin' tuh commit suicide,' said Corey. He eased his mount gently forward. Both horses began to canter.

The sounds came nearer. Three horsemen suddenly loomed up out of the night.

Butch could have *hurrooed* with relief. But he just shouted, 'Hullo, boys.'

'It's Butch,' came the welcome voice of Red McGrath. 'He's got another feller with him.'

Butch brought his gun to light again. 'Yeh,' he said. 'Better watch this feller. He's a real snake.'

Corey spoke then, his tones surprised. 'Jack Berners! I didn't think you'd be a member of the gang.'

'Corey!' echoed Berners. 'What's the matter, Butch? This man's an old friend o' mine.'

'Wal, he ain't no friend o' mine,' snarled Butch harshly.

The sudden burst of anger seemed to suddenly weaken him. He slumped a little in the saddle.

Slip Anderson rode forward. 'You hurt, Butch?'

'Yeh, jest creased in the side. I've lost a lotta blood tho'.'

Red had his gun out. 'See tuh Butch, Slip,' he said. 'I'll drill this *hombre* if he tries anythin'.' He spoke out of the corner of his mouth to Berners. 'He might be a pal o' yourn, Jack, but he's suttinly got some explainin' tuh do.'

'Yeh, I guess so,' agreed Berners.

'I told yuh them wuz shots we heard,' said Slip. He was supporting Butch in the saddle. 'Big boy here ain't in none too grand shape. We'd better get back to the grove, pronto.'

'Don't waste too much time,' said Butch. 'I guess there's a mob out after us by now.'

Red spoke to Jim Corey. 'Move out in front, pardner. Get goin'.'

Silently the saloon-man did as he was told. Jack Berners moved with him.

'Keep by me a mite, Jack,' said Red. There was an edge on his voice.

Berners shrugged in the darkness. 'I jest wanted to get the drift. I guess Corey thinks we are the other three bozos who did the hold-up in Sarido.'

'I guess he does,' said Red softly. 'Purty soon he'll hafta tell us all about it. He'll hafta do plenty o' talkin' to explain the shape Butch is in.'

In silence they reached the grove of trees where Butch's brown stallion, the indirect cause of all the ruckus, was tethered to a tree, champing grass patiently.

'So yuh found him,' said the big man. 'Yeh, we found the durned critter,' said Slip. 'Light down, pardner, an' c'mon over here.' He helped Butch from his horse and led him to the dying embers of the fire. The big man slumped down. Slip knelt and quickly blew the embers to a tiny blaze. He added more sticks. Pretty soon he had quite a sizeable fire. Butch was grateful for the sudden warmth.

Slip said: 'We'll have to take a chance for a bit. Keep your ears open, fellers, in case Mr So-an-so's friends spot the light an' come a-ridin'.'

'You won't have much chance if they do,' said Corey levelly.

'Shet your trap,' Red snarled. 'Light down. An' watch yourself.'

Corey dismounted and crossed to the fire where Slip with bandage from his saddle-bag was binding Butch's wound. It was nasty but not very bad. The blood was effectively staunched now but the big man was likely to be mighty sore for a few weeks.

When Slip had finished, Butch thanked him and rose to his feet, flexing his big muscles.

He still felt kind of unsteady. He sat down again. 'I'll live,' he said.

Slip began to make coffee. Jim Corey sat down a little way from the fire. He rested his back against the slim trunk of a cottonwood. Red squatted a short distance away from him. The firelight glinting on the barrel of the Colt held slackly between his knees, reflected the brilliance of his blue eyes as he watched the saloon-man dispassionately, but with a subtle menace.

Jack Berners crossed over from tethering the horses and, getting down on one knee before the fire, began to warm his hands.

Butch began to tell his tale. Corey tried to break in a few times but was again told by Red to shut his trap. When Butch had finished it was Jack Berners who spoke, turning towards the saloon-man as he did so.

'It looks like yuh got the wrong man this time, Jim,' he said. 'We're after the same three guys that you are. We trailed 'em from up in the Pecos.'

'I took my men's word that he was the big feller who helped to hold up my place,' said Corey sullenly. He seemed only half-convinced.

'You know me,' said Berners tersely. 'You can take my word that he ain't.'

'He put paid to quite a few of my men.'

'I didn't start the jamboree,' broke in Butch. 'They asked for all they got. I might've bin a dead pigeon myself by now. I'm the injured party not you.'

'Seems to me he's right, mister,' said Red drily. 'I guess we'd be quite justified in stringing you up on that cottonwood agin which you're leanin'.'

Corey figured he'd better change his tune. A gambler all his life he knew when he was licked. Right now he was badgered and hogtied.

He said: 'Well, gentlemen, if I made a

mistake I apologize. Actually it was the mistake of two of my men. I reckon they've adequately paid for it.' He looked straight at Butch. 'They didn't come up out o' the cellar did they?'

'One of 'em won't,' said Butch. 'I don't know about the other.'

'You figure they've paid then?' Corey was the cool gambler now, counting the odds and the losses.

'I guess they have,' said Butch.

The saloon-owner bowed slightly. 'Then I apologize for my own mistake. If I must pay too, well,' he spread his hands and shrugged. 'I'm in your hands, gentlemen. I will add however,' he continued, shooting his bolt home, 'that if we part amicably you are welcome in Sarido and you will not be molested.'

Butch looked enquiringly at Jack Berners. 'I think he's on the level,' said the latter. Corey bowed again. 'Thank you, Jack.'

'You're welcome, I guess. I owe yuh a spin.'

Suddenly Butch grinned. 'I accept your apology,' he said.

In the shadows Red began to laugh softly. Squatting on his haunches, staring into the fire with his mouth half-open, Slip Anderson seemed to have lost all interest in the proceedings. But it was he who suddenly rose to his feet and said laconically:

'There's hosses comin'.'

In an instant all present were on their feet. Red, Butch, and Jack all with swiftly-drawn guns in their fists. Corey rose with them. He, of course, was unarmed. Slip chucked half a canful of coffee over the fire. It hissed and spluttered, sending up clouds of steam. It was effectively doused.

Judging by the sounds in the wind there was a sizeable bunch of horsemen and although they were yet quite a distance away they seemed to be making straight for the spot where the five men stood. And coming fast, too.

Jim Corey said: 'It's probably my men. If you'll leave this to me, gentlemen, and trust me, I'll handle them.'

'Wal, I guess I'd sooner stay than make a break for it now,' drawled Slip. 'But I'll keep my gun ready.' He drew it nonchalantly.

Butch said: 'That goes for all of us. You'd better walk a little way in front an' wait for the visitors, Mr Corey.'

The saloon-man shrugged and began to walk forward. 'That's enough,' said Butch. 'Jest stay there where we can see yuh.'

Corey half-turned. 'Don't yuh trust me . . . ?'

'Yeh, yeh, we trust yuh.' Butch grinned again. 'But these visitors might not be your men. If they are, wal, all you've got to do is yell at 'em as soon as they see yuh. Be sure you yell before we start shooting. Don't forget you're right in the line of fire.'

Corey turned his back on them, silently, his shoulders set squarely. Maybe he was offended. Butch kept on grinning, standing with his back to the hissing remains of the fire. Beside him Jack Berners was silent and grim-faced, his own gun ready. Slip drew alongside them. Red took a few paces nearer to Corey and got behind a tree. He would have the best view of the saloon-owner and the oncoming riders and could watch developments closely. He had both his guns out.

The five men waited as the hoofbeats became clearer. There was little doubt in anybody's mind now that the riders had seen the fire and were making straight for the grove.

The ground trembled with the reverberations of thudding hooves. The first riders came in view. Then Corey raised his arms and yelled: 'Hold it, boys. It's me.'

'The boss,' yelled somebody.

Then: 'That you, boss?'

'Yeh, it's me. I've got some friends here. Keep your hands away from your guns an' ride in slowly. They're mighty jumpy in here.'

'What's the matter, boss?'

'Don't ask questions,' shouted Corey, hoarsely. 'Do as I say.'

By his voice and manner it was hard to tell whether he was really playing it straight or just doing it to be on the safe side. From behind the tree Red watched the horsemen ride nearer, slowly. He counted thirteen of them. An unlucky number. But unlucky for whom?

# 8

## 1

Sarido was a hell-roaring wide-open town, familiar with homicide and the other more refined sins to no small measure, but the night on which the big man with spectacles shot up Corey's Palace was certainly one in a million. One to remember till the end, to recount over and over again.

The lanky Dink was dead with his skull broken in pieces. His ugly pard, Jugger, also had a cracked skull, plus busted ribs, but he would probably survive. One of the bartenders was dead. He'd been hit in the stomach and died slowly, regaining consciousness once to scream in an agonized delirium which chilled the hearts of the hardest. Besides him and Dink there were three other dead men. And two wounded,

Jugger making three. The big feller had certainly made his presence felt. And taken King Corey with him to boot. Many already counted the dictator of Sarido as good as dead. Whether he was mourned or not was a moot point and, though nobody broached it aloud, open to speculation.

The rather belated posse had left, the bodies had been carted away to the funeral parlour, the wounded were being treated by the town's one and only, and habitually drunken, medico. The populace to a man, and the women too, packed itself into the Palace and swopped yarns. Whiskey ran like the water in a pebbly creek. The men told of what they'd've done to the big feller if so-and-so or something hadn't been in the way. The percentage-girls egged them on and made a real good thing out of it all.

In contrast to the Palace and its immediate vicinity the rest of Sarido was silent and, except for occasional cowboys, bound as a rule in the same direction, it was empty too. Those of the populace who could not get to the bar in the Palace or who for some reason or other preferred other places, were gathered in one or another of the dozen or so gambling-houses, eating-joints and brothels which abounded in this border midden. The ordinary stores were dark and shuttered and most of the few cabins. The majority of the populace slept in the lodging houses or above the different sporting establishments.

Where the street curved to rise into the Mexican hills three horsemen were descending the slope. The night was very dark and they were but vague figures in the gloom. They did not ride straight into the street but deviated so that they were approaching the buildings from the side. Their progress was strangely silent. They halted close to the dark shack which was the first building in the street. In the gloom their horses' hooves looked enormous. They were bound with sacking: another one of

Ginger's bright ideas. He knew all the tricks. It was he who spoke first in familiar, snarling tones.

He said: 'The gunsmith's is the nearest. We'll take that first. He's an old guy. He's probably fast asleep. You know what to do. Lafe, you stay outside an' keep watch. Me an' Monty'll go in. Be as quiet as possible. No shootin' unless it's absolutely necessary.'

The fat man nodded. 'All right, Ginger,' he said. Lafe just grunted surlily.

'C'mon then,' said Ginger. He dismounted from his horse and led the way round the backs of the houses. The others followed suit.

Presently Ginger halted. 'This is it,' he said.

Monty said: 'They all look alike tuh me.'

Ginger wasn't amused. He snarled: 'I know this is it . . . C'mon . . . Watch the hosses, Lafe. Keep your eyes an' ears peeled.'

Lafe did not speak. He bunched the

horses together. He had been kind of at loggerheads with Ginger lately. They did not seem to see eye to eye. Ginger was a damnsight too bossy lately. Lafe didn't like it. Right now he didn't argue. He was just as keen to pull this job off as Ginger was, but he didn't understand why he had been chosen to stand around with the hosses while fat clumsy Monty went inside. It was asking for trouble. Anyway, he told himself sardonically, if anything did pop he'd make durned sure of making a getaway himself, and to hell with the other two.

Ginger tried the windows at the back of the place. They were tightly fastened. Monty, gun in hand, and with a shapeless something tucked under his arm dogged the redhead's footsteps. Ginger tried the door. It was stoutly made and obviously locked, bolted and barred.

Ginger returned to one of the windows. 'Gimme that sack, Monty,' he said. The fat man handed over the shapeless something.

Ginger took the sack, wrapped it around his fist and with one sharp blow, broke the window. He handed the sack again to Monty and inserted his hand in the aperture he had made. The catch slipped back, the window was opened.

'I'll go first,' hissed the redhead. 'Watch yourself.'

He clambered lithely through the window. After a moment Monty followed. He landed inside with a bump and Ginger cursed him in a choked whisper.

Lafe heard the bump too and grinned crookedly. Ginger had only taken the big lummox with him out of spite. Serve him right if they came unstuck. He looked about him. It was mighty quiet. There wasn't likely to be anybody coming around unless Monty woke somebody up to give the alarm.

A light blossomed inside the stores as Ginger struck a match. 'C'mon,' he hissed. Monty followed him through another door.

'Right across,' said Ginger. 'Easy.'

Pretty soon they were in the store proper. Ginger struck another match. He looked around him quickly, ferret-like.

'Guns and shells over there,' he said, pointing. 'Get plenty o' shells — an' a Winchester. Take it easy fer Chris'sake. Don't knock anything over.'

'All right,' mumbled Monty.

'Get over there,' said Ginger. 'As soon as you're fixed I'm going back into this middle place and close the door. Lie low until I fetch yuh.'

Monty weaved his bulk across the floor of the store. Ginger watched him until he was safely in position. Then he stepped back into the middle place and closed the door gently behind him. He struck another match and looked around.

He spotted what he sought; a hurricane lantern hanging from a beam in the ceiling. He crossed to it and lit it.

The place revealed was an office-cum-living room. There was a battered rolltop desk with a rickety chair before it. On a small deal table were the remains of a meal. The rest of the furniture consisted of a sofa and three chairs. The floor was bare boards with a few worn mats strewn across it. To the left of Ginger as he stood facing the desk was another door. The redhead knew that beyond there slept the old storekeeper and his youthful assistant.

Ginger had heard the storekeeper was an old miser. 'Twas said he had a fortune stacked away somewhere in his establishment and slept with a loaded, sawn-off shotgun beside his bed. It'd be too bad for somebody if he spotted the light.

Ginger was clear-headed, he didn't take any desperate chances. He decided what he must do. He turned off the light again. Then he got down on his hands and knees and, gun in hand, began to crawl towards the door.

He reached up and lifted the latch.

Then he pressed himself against the wall beside the door and with one hand pushed the door open. Nothing happened. From somewhere in the blackness beyond came the sound of asthmatical snoring. Ginger wormed his way through the half-opened door and began to crawl again. Finally, he came up against the cold metal leg of some bedsteads. He stopped, holding his breath. From up above him the snoring continued unabated.

Ginger rose to his feet and walked round to the head of the bed. He reached in his jeans, got a match and struck it on the butt of the gun he held in his other hand. It lit up the emaciated, yellow features of the old man who lay in the bed. Ginger lowered the flame until it was poised above the old man's nose.

The eyelids opened slowly. The old eyes were bleary, the whites showing unpleasantly. The pupils distended suddenly with terror. A withered arm shot from beneath the bed clothes, reaching for the gun beside the bed, the toothless mouth opened.

Ginger touched the old man's face with the cold steel barrel of his Colt.

'Hold it,' he said, 'or I'll blow your brains out.'

The old mouth closed like a trap. The hand wavered. 'Let's have both your mitts on top o' the bedclothes, said Ginger.

The old man did as he was told. 'What do you want?' he quavered.

The match burnt out. Ginger dropped it. Now both faces were mere blobs in the gloom. Ginger pressed the gun-barrel harder against the wrinkled skin.

'I jest want you to answer a few questions,' he whispered. 'An' quietly, very quietly. Remember I've only got to hit you once across the haid with this an' you'll be a gonner.'

'What do you want?' said the storekeeper again. His voice was thin and reedy. He sounded like a child repeating a lesson. Ginger could feel him trembling and felt cruel, savage satisfaction. This was going to be easy.

'First of all,' he said. 'Where's your assistant?'

'He sleeps in the loft in the stables.'

'Where's that?'

'Jest the back of here.'

'Which way would he hafta come to get in here?'

'Through the back door.'

'You're not lying tuh me?' snarled Ginger, pressing harder with a gun.

'No, mister, no!'

'You take awful chances ol' man,' said the other, 'sleeping here all alone like yuh do. I guess you wouldn't want your assistant to know all your business tho' would yuh? You wouldn't like him creeping around of nights maybe, ferretting things out.'

The old man did not speak. His breathing was laboured, there was a little whistle in his throat. Ginger caressed the parchment-like flesh gently with the barrel of the gun. The other's trembling became uncontrollable.

'Wh-what do you want?' he said

again, parrot-like. 'I'm poor, I've got no money for you. If it's guns you want there are plenty in the shop. Help yourself.'

'We are,' chuckled Ginger.

'Well, I've got nothing else I . . . ' His voice was rising in terror. Ginger tapped him sharply with the gun. 'Quietly' he snarled.

The old man began to cough. Ginger pressed cruelly with the gun. The flesh broke, blood ran. The old man gave a little snort of pain and stopped coughing.

When he spoke again his voice was a choked whisper, tremulous, and hardly audible. 'That's better,' said Ginger.

The old man repeated over and over, 'What do you want? What do you want . . . ?' Then he found a more coherent tongue and said: 'I've got nuthin' for yuh. I'm a pore ol' man. Everybody knows me. I don't do anybody any harm. I jest sell me guns and stuff. Nobody bothers me.'

'Dear, dear,' said Ginger. 'I feel real

sorry for yuh. I told yuh I only came for a little chat.' His voice became thicker. The old man winced as the gun barrel bit into his wounded cheek once more. Ginger continued passionately. 'A quick talk I wanted. We've wasted too much time over it already. You know what I want, yuh money-countin' ol' buzzard. Where is it?'

The old man's trembling made the bed creak. The watching gunman could vaguely see the palpitating clawlike hands on top of the counterpane. The owner babbled in a cracked whisper: 'Where's what? I don't know what you mean.'

Ginger lost his temper. His voice became louder. 'Don't stall, damn yuh. Your money. Where is it? I know you've got it stacked away somewheres . . . ' He stopped, realizing he was talking too loud. To relieve his feelings he gave the man in the bed another crack with the gun, making him sob with terror and pain. He bent his face closer and whispered conversationally.

'You'd better start talkin' ol' timer. I cain't waste much more time. I've got an urgent appointment. I'll give you a coupla minutes then if you don't talk I'm gonna tap you lightly on the bean, just enough to keep yuh quiet for a bit, then I'm gonna set the place alight. Which is the most precious to you, your life or your money? It ain't pleasant tuh be roasted alive yuh know.'

Very sure of himself was Ginger, and he had a great sense of the dramatic. The burning part of it had only just occurred to him as something to terrify the old man into loosening his tongue, but already he could see its possibilities. Why not? While the fire was attracting the populace he and his two men could clean up all around town.

## 2

Monty crouched in the shop and waited. He had already filled the sack with all they needed. Ginger was taking a hell of a while. The fat man couldn't see far in the gloom and characteristically he had already lost his sense of direction. He was scared to strike another light in case it was spotted from outside. Anyway, Ginger had said for him to stay put. He could only squat there and wait for the door to open. But the waiting was beginning to get on his nerves.

Lafe didn't *have* any nerves but, waiting outside with the horses, the inactivity was beginning to chafe him, adding fuel every second to his smouldering resentment against Ginger. What was he doing all this time? What was he doing now? Something he considered very, very clever no doubt.

A door or window creaked and Lafe was alert in an instant. Maybe it was the other two returning, but, somehow, Lafe did not think so. The sound seemed to come from the side of the building somewhere; nowhere near the window through which Ginger and Monty had broken in.

Lafe left the horses and went back into the gloom a little. Then he began to make a detour, calculating it to bring him out at a point near where he figured the sound had come from. He began to move in.

He came out by the stables. A dark form was worming its way from the open doorway there and around the corner of the house. Lafe, gun ready, crept closer. Pretty soon he could see that the other was only a younker. But he carried a gun in his paw, and didn't look unused to it either. Gunplay was the last thing Lafe wanted.

He crossed to the stable without being seen. The youth's attention was all in front. Lafe pressed himself against the frame-wall, the stable was attached to the main building, and began to follow in the other's wake.

He was almost upon his quarry when one of his spurs clinked against the boardwall. The youth whirled as Lafe leapt, his gun swinging in an arc. It caught the youth with terrific force on the side of the head. But his finger was already squeezing the trigger. As he crumpled the gun boomed deafeningly, the slug ploughed up the dirt at Lafe's feet. The latter gave the prostrate form a vicious kick then ran for the horses.

In the bedroom Ginger heard the shot. He cursed. The old man jerked upwards. Ginger hit him across the head with the barrel of the gun. He slumped. Ginger left him.

But he reckoned not with the toughness of the old buzzard. He was going through the door when the shotgun boomed. Buckshot screamed. But the old man's hands were trembling, his eyes could not see in the dark. The wall was peppered. A stray piece stung Ginger's thigh. He turned, levelling his gun, pressing the trigger savagely, pumping lead into the darkness. Then he turned into the other room.

He could hear Monty blundering about frenziedly in the shop. He flung open the door.

'Here!' he shouted. 'Quickly, you fool!'

Monty joined him. Lafe was already mounted when they got outside. He urged his horse forward. But the other two were not far behind him. Down-town excited voices were raised. Hell sure was poppin' in Sarido tonight!

The three miscreants skirted the buildings and began to ascend the slope. People were not far behind them. A man ran from one of the houses at the end of the street. He carried a rifle. He raised it and sighted coolly at the runaways. He fired.

Ginger's horse gave a convulsive shudder, then buckled at the knees, throwing its rider over its head. The other two galloped on.

Ginger staggered to his feet. 'Lafe! Monty!' he screamed.

Monty checked his horse, so accus-tomed was he to obeying Ginger's voice. Lafe raised his gun meaningly. 'Keep moving,' he said.

Monty looked at him. Lafe grinned,

his eyes gleaming. Monty urged his horse forward again.

Ginger began to run up the slope, shaking his fist after them, mouthing curses.

Horsemen were thundering up the street behind him. He continued to run but he knew he was trapped. There was no cover, no hope!

As the horsemen began to climb the slope he turned, his teeth bared like a wild animal at bay, and began shooting with both guns.

A volley answered him. Many slugs hit him. As he began to buckle at the knees he screamed at them, sheer savage guts keeping his guns in line, his fingers still pressing the triggers. More than one of the horsemen tumbled from his mount. But suddenly the devilish twin guns were silent and their owner pitched on his face. His body came bouncing down the slope to rest at the feet of their horses.

Another bunch of horsemen were riding in at the other end of town. At their head was Jim Corey, bareheaded, and beside him, Jack Berners.

They heard the shooting and urged their horses forward. People came running down the street towards them, recognized Corey, with surprise maybe, and began to shout the news.

Finally, some sense was culled from the babble.

'It's the three *hombres* we're after,' said Berners.

Corey said: 'Wal, I guess I really owe you an apology, Jack.'

'Forget it,' Berners turned in the saddle as his three pards joined him. 'You heard?'

'Yeh,' said Butch. 'What are we waiting for?'

He broke away first. The other three thundered after them.

'Go with them, some of you,' said Corey. 'Stay with them.'

About half-a-dozen of his men detached themselves from the main body and followed the quartet.

Red looked back. 'Looks like Mr

Corey still don't trust us,' he said.

Slip said: 'And then again maybe he only wants tuh help. It's his town that's bin shot up yuh know. We'd better wait for 'em.'

They eased their mounts and let the others catch up.

'The boss says we wuz tuh help yuh,' said the foremost rider.

'Sure. It's your territory,' said Slip.

The whole party swept past the knot of people that was gathered round the body of Ginger.

'He's deader'n mackerel!' yelled somebody.

'Pity,' said Red laconically. 'I should've liked to've taken him myself.'

Cheek-by-jowl with their erstwhile enemies — or were they *still* enemies? — the four pards rode on upwards to the craggy heights above. All were silent now. Horses and men were used to the wilds and they followed almost instinctively, a faintly discernible trail. But this did not last. Pretty soon they found themselves in real fastnesses and undecided which course to take.

'Purty hopeless hunting around here after dark like this,' said one of Corey's men. 'We might get plumb lost. It'd be better tuh go back tuh town an' try an' pick up the trail in the mornin'.' Judging by his weary, disgruntled tones he evidently had had enough of gallivanting about for one night.

They halted on a wide slab of rock. ''Pears tuh me we've come the wrong way anyway,' said Slip Anderson. 'The going's getting harder every minute. I guess no hoss could get up above there.'

'I'm all for goin' back,' said another of the Corey men. There were murmurs from the others. They seemed disinterested one way or the other. They had not, like the partners, any personal grudges to work off. They seemed quite complacent and unwarlike.

'You boys go back then,' said Slip. 'We'll hang on a bit. Maybe we'll bivouac up here. We've got a particular reason for meeting up with them two stickup men.'

It was an almost direct challenge to the Corey mob. Red, for one, dropped his hand to the butt of his gun. Now he guessed they'd know what were the intentions of the King of Sarido.

'Yeh, c'mon let's go,' said the first Corey man. 'If these *hombres* want tuh hang on up here it's their funeral.' But as he spoke he was looking at the biggest man of his own bunch, the one Jack Berners knew to be called Strangler, and who was one of Corey's righthand men. Everybody looked at Strangler.

Red was all set to drill the feller right through his big head if he tried anything funny. But Strangler was merely pondering. Finally he said, in a very deep, hoarse voice, 'Wal, yes, maybe we had better go back. I guess the boss wouldn't want us tuh keep ridin' an' ridin'.' He turned his head in the direction of Slip. 'Ain't you fellers comin'? The boss said you'd be welcome.'

'Yeh, we know,' said Slip, who was

doing a lot of talking for one night. 'But I guess we'll hang on. At dawn we'll try an' pick up the trail. Maybe we could meet you boys then. You git back an' git some rest an' don't worry 'bout us.'

Strangler was no match for the lean runny's smooth tongue.

'All right,' he mumbled. 'See you in the mornin'.' He turned his horse's head. His men followed suit. The four pardners watched them until the misty darkness swallowed them up.

'Phew!' said Red. 'I had a notion things might start jumping any minute.'

Jack Berners said: 'I guess Corey don't mean us any harm now, but jest wants to keep tabs on us. Maybe Strangler'll get a bawling-out fer leavin' the trail. Still, he obviously didn't mean to stick his neck out.'

Butch was sore and tired and a little peeved. He said: 'Wal, what'll we do now? I guess Slip was right when he said hosses cain't climb up there. I guess we've got to turn back too.'

'Nothin' else for it,' Slip agreed. 'But

there was no sense in riding meekly back to Sarido with that bunch. Corey may still have somep'n up his sleeve.'

All present were aware of the probability of this fact. Even Jack Berners was moved to say that Corey was a mighty slippery and unpredictable customer.

They turned and began to descend the treacherous slopes. They found rest finally lower down in the dubious shelter of an outcrop of stunted shrubs which overhung another ledge. They dare not light a fire for fear of giving away their position. They composed themselves as best they could — not without, however, a modicum of grumbling and cursing, and prepared themselves for an uncomfortable night.

Jack Berners elected to go down into town again and reconnoitre. He suited himself. He set off on foot.

'I guess if Corey's intentions are still warlike he won't be quite so nasty with me if I'm caught,' he said before he left. 'But I won't get spotted unless I can help it. I'll get back as soon as I can with whatever news I can pick up.'

## 3

The log-cabin was a one-roomed, sagging-roofed affair with a dirt floor. The furniture consisted of a rickety deal table, and two packing-cases. Against the far wall, facing the sagging door and narrow broken window was a low bunk laid with dirty, tattered blankets. Near to another wall was a cracked, pot-bellied stove with a rusty pipe which soared crazily upwards and disappeared through a jagged hole in the roof. The stove was alight.

The door crashed open, kicked forcibly by a heavy riding-boot. Lafe stepped inside carrying an armful of small logs. Behind him lumbered Monty similarly laden. They dropped the stuff beside the stove and Lafe began to stoke it up. He said: 'Open that can of pork an' beans and get some coffee brewed.'

Monty crossed to a corner where saddle gear, bags and blankets were carelessly jumbled together, rummaged for a bit then brought forth the desired articles. Also a couple of tin mugs. From the pocket of his jeans he produced a jacknife. He rose and placed the can of pork and beans and the tin of coffee on the table.

'Where's the pot?' he said.

Lafe reached behind the stove and brought forth a blackened saucepan. He handed this back to his companion.

'I'll go get some water,' the fat man said.

Lafe grunted. Monty left the place.

Lafe turned. He picked up the jacknife from the table, snapped it open, and attacked the can with it. Monty returned with the water. He placed it on the top of the stove, which was now roaring merrily. Then he turned, picked up his knife, and replaced it in his pocket.

Lafe looked at him and showed his snaggle-teeth in a grin.

Monty said: 'We oughta to've gone back for Ginger. We'd've got him all right.'

'Yuh know we shouldn't've,' said Lafe in quite friendly tones. 'We both would be dead pigeons like him if we'd gone back. Quit worryin' I tell yuh. We're sitting pretty. Nobody'll find us here — the prospector who built this must've bin plumb crazy but it suttinly is a swell hideout . . . An' remember,' he added slyly, 'we've only got to split the swag two ways now.'

Monty's little eyes lit up with an avaricious light. Maybe his slow-thinking brain had not tumbled to that fact before. He did not speak.

'C'mon, let's have some chow,' said Lafe. 'Quit worryin'. We'll get on all right without Ginger, he wasn't the only one with brains . . . As for me I don't think this country's worth the pickin'. I want to get where a man can live properly. I'm headin' back to the States as soon as I can. What d'yuh say, Monty?'

'I'm with yuh,' said the fat man. He looked quite cheerful now. Ol' Lafe wasn't such a bad feller really an' not so disagreeable as Ginger had been. He'd stick by Lafe. Shore thing! An' that extra swag. That share was a good point. No, he guessed he wasn't gonna shed no tears over Ginger.

He lumbered about like a huge fussy dog, helping Lafe get the supper.

Half-an-hour later, when the chow had been consumed and the dirty utensils chucked into a corner, they sat opposite each other across the table.

Lafe said: 'Wal, I guess now is as good a time as any to divide the swag. The sooner I get out o' this pesky country the better I'll like it.'

'Yeh,' said Monty, grinning friendly-like. 'Yeh, sure.'

'You get it then,' said Lafe. 'You're nearest.'

Monty left his packing case seat and crossed to the bunk. He got down on his hands and knees and brought forth from a dark corner a gunny sack. Lafe watched his broad flabby back with a little smile on his wizened young-old face. The smile was still there when Monty turned and slung the sack on to the table.

Lafe caught hold of the sack, and unhurriedly untied the strings at its mouth. Monty sat down again and watched his partner with eager eyes, his blubbery mouth half-open. A cascade of green notes and shining silver coins shimmered and crackled on to the table, spreading and growing, a little mountain of pure wealth.

Monty put out a plump hand. Lafe said 'ah-ah,' and slapped it gently. The fat man drew it away, pouting like a child who had been chided.

He watched Lafe's sinewy claws come forward and, methodically, with no trace of hurry and nervousness split the pile into two sections. One section he drew to himself, the other he pushed across the table to Monty. The latter pile was by far the smallest.

Monty's eyes looked surprised. He

couldn't figure what his pardner was playing at. He said: 'We have tuh count it don't we?'

Lafe looked up. His face was expressionless. He said carelessly, 'Aw, I don't think that's necessary. That'll be near enough.'

Monty looked pained. 'Your pile's a mite bigger'n mine,' he said.

Lafe said: 'Aw, don't let a little thing like that worry you. I didn't think you'd quibble over a little thing like that. Anyway, now I'm the brains of the outfit I ought to have the biggest share.'

Monty wasn't all that dumb. If it came to that why shouldn't *he* have the biggest share. His piggy eyes drooped. His hand slid below the table.

Even as he drew his gun, Lafe rose swiftly to his feet, his own gun in his hand, and struck out. The gun barrel slashed Monty across the temple, splitting it wide open. The fat man went over backwards and lay still. The whites of his eyes gazed up at the ceiling. Blood gushed from his wound.

Lafe walked round the table and bent over him. He reached into the pocket of the unconscious man's jeans and brought forth the jacknife. He opened it and ran his thumb experimentally along the long blade. He nodded with satisfaction.

His movements were quite deliberate. He raised the knife and brought it down with terrific force in Monty's breast. Four times he did this, grunting with the exertion. Then he was satisfied. He left the knife in the body.

He rose and opened the door. Then he dragged the body outside and left it there.

He gathered up the money from the table and stowed it back into the gunny-sack, smiling as he did so. He shoved the sack back underneath the bunk. He took off his gunbelt and slung it on the table. But he removed his gun and put it under the dirty pillow on the bunk. Then he took off his boots and fully dressed as he was blew out the lamp and climbed in between the tattered blankets. He'd take his chance at dawn rather than risk the mountains at night. In a few minutes he was asleep.

At that same time Jack Berners was brought to an abrupt stop on a dark boardwalk in Sarido by the sudden jab of a gun-barrel in the small of his back.

'Git moving, feller,' said a low hoarse voice. 'Git into the light an' see the boss. Right now he's mighty suspicious o' folks snoopin' around.'

Berners realized there were two men. Both of them had guns trained at his spine. He shrugged and allowed them to shepherd him along an alley to the backs of houses. He knew where they were making for.

His surmise proved correct for pretty soon he was facing Jim Corey in his office.

'All right, boys,' said the boss. 'You can put your guns away.' He eyed Berners quizzically. 'You could've come in openly, Jack. Nobody would've bothered you. I keep my word. I've got no quarrel with you or your friends.'

'That's what I came to find out.'

'Well, now you know . . . However,' added Corey. 'I should not advise your big pard to come riding in. The boys he rubbed out had friends here who might like to even-up the score. And they wouldn't be particular how they did it either.'

'I'll tell Butch that,' said Berners. 'In fact I guess I'd better be ridin' back now.'

'Don't be in such an all-fired hurry,' said Corey. 'You're my guest now. Stay and have supper with me.'

Berners figured there couldn't be any harm in doing that anyway. The boys wouldn't expect him back yet awhile.

So they sat and supped and talked over old times. It was nearly two o'clock in the morning when Jack was conducted to a spare room over the Palace by his old pal and buddy, Jim. Both men were lit-up more than somewhat.

Jack managed to get his boots and his neckerchief off then he tumbled like a log on to the bed. In a few seconds he was snoring lustily.

When he awoke the morning sun was filtering through the window. Gosh, he was late. He sprang out of bed. Luckily he never suffered with hangovers.

He scrambled into his boots, tied his neckerchief hurriedly, buckled on his gunbelt. The boys would be wondering what had happened to him. He crammed his hat on his tousled head and made for the door. His hand was on the latch when he heard hoofbeats outside. Maybe that was the boys coming after him. If it was he must warn Butch pronto. They seemed to be stopping out front. There seemed to be more than three horses, however. His room was at the back of the saloon so he could not look out of the window to investigate.

He flung open the door and clattered down the stairs. He walked along the passage to the door which led into the bar room. He opened it and stepped through. One of the barmen was sprinkling sawdust on the boards.

He turned his head and said: 'Mornin'.'

'Mornin',' said Berners. He passed the man and lifted the trap to pass beyond the bar. He turned to fasten the trap securely behind him. He heard the batwings open and turned again. On the threshold of the bar room stood Marshal Max Winters of El Paso.

The two sworn enemies spotted each other simultaneously. Winters was alone but the sound of thudding boot-heels on the boardwalk denoted that his men were not far behind him.

'Berners!' he said.

The other man did not speak. He just moved a few paces across the floor and half crouched, his arms dangling. All the furniture had been pushed against the walls for the convenience of the barman and his perambulations with the sawdust-bucket. There was a clear space between the two men.

'My men are outside, Berners,' said Winters. 'You haven't got a chance.' He wasn't scared. Just his usual wary self.

Berners did not answer him. He just smiled. But the smile did not reach his eyes. They were cold. They looked through the marshal and beyond him.

Winters shrugged, bent a little, his hands swooping downwards. Both men were very fast. The sawdust-johnny dived for cover behind his bar as the heavy Colts boomed.

Winters spun round as a slug bit into the fleshy part of his shoulders. He regained his balance and seemed to rebound, lurching forward. Berners left leg went from under him as the kneecap was smashed. Another slug took his hat off. He stayed on one knee, his head thrust forward, his teeth bared, throwing slugs from both guns at the tall figure before him in the smoke and the din. His eyes stung with cordite so that he could hardly see but a savage exultation filled his heart as he saw the vague tall figure wilting like a broken derrick. Then he could see no more and all was smoke and nightmare and searing pain. Then a giant fist smote him in the chest. He went backwards, fighting all the time. Then forward again to collapse coughing, on his face, his forehead hitting the bare hard boards of the floor.

Slowly the man with the bucket rose from behind his bar. The echoes had died away leaving a horrid void of silence. The smoke was clearing. The stink of cordite filled the air. In the middle of the bar room, barely four yards away from each other, lay two still crumpled figures.

The batwings opened slowly, members of the marshal's band began to filter in. They had their guns out.

The bartender licked dry lips. 'The party's over, boys,' he said weakly.

He looked ludicrous standing in the open trap of the bar, whisk-brush and bucket held in his hands. The boys gaped at him. The foremost holstered his gun and, stepping forward bent over the marshal. At the same instant Jim Corey came through the door behind the bar. He carried a sawn-off shotgun.

Half-a-dozen Colts were instantly lev-elled at him.

'All right, boys,' he said. 'I own this place. Looks like the shooting's all finished. You can put away your hardware.'

'The marshal's daid!'

'Marshal, eh?' said Corey. 'Max Winters?'

'Yeh.'

Corey turned to the barman. 'How'd it happen?'

The man's rubicund face was begin-ning to regain its natural ruddiness. He snapped his fingers. 'Like that,' he said. 'They spotted each other an' started blastin' pronto.'

One of the other men spoke. 'Winters wuz after him. An' his three pards.'

'Where're his pards?' said somebody else.

Corey ignored the question. He came round the bar and got down on his knees beside Berners. He turned him over and raised his head in the crook of his arm.

'Finished?' said the barman.

Corey nodded. He took a white silk handkerchief and began to wipe the bloody froth from around Berner's lips. The barman watched with mingled feelings. It was hard to figure the boss sometimes. Fancy him fussing over a broken-down saddle-tramp thataway.

# 9

## 1

The three pardners were descending the hillside to look for Jack when they heard the shots, the sounds floating up the slopes to them and fading away in the fastnesses behind with spectral whispering echoes.

'Somethin's happenin',' said Butch and spurred his horse forward.

'Easy,' said Slip, 'it won't do to ride straight intah town like that. We'd best make a detour an' come out at the backs like we said.'

'Yeh, I guess you're right,' said Butch. They left the trail.

'If anythin's happened to Jack, Corey's gonna wish he'd never bin born,' said Red savagely.

They got into Sarido and the back of the Palace without mishap. Corey was reclining in his swivel-chair when Butch kicked the office door open. The saloon-owner faced the three men with their drawn guns. His black eyes were expressionless, his hands were placed on top of the desk before him.

Butch said: 'Where's Jack Berners?'

'Yeh,' said Red savagely, 'If anything's happened tuh Jack you got some real fast talkin' to do, mister.'

Corey's voice was as expressionless as his face when he said: 'Jack Berners is dead.'

'Damn you,' snarled the volatile redhead. With quick, jerky steps he went nearer to the desk, his gun levelled at the saloon-man's breast. His eyes blazed, his face was white.

'Hold it, Red,' said Slip.

Red halted. His finger was curled around the trigger of his gun, the ball of his thumb was poised on the hammer; he glared at Corey.

The saloon owner knew that with the least pressure the gun would blast searing death. He did not flinch.

He said: 'I didn't kill Jack Berners. He was my friend. Marshal Max Winters of El Paso and his men came into town. Winters and Jack had a gun battle. Winters is dead too.' As the three men watched him he rose. 'Jack's body is upstairs. I'll take you if you like.'

'All right,' said Red. Surprised tho' he was to hear about Winters, and shocked at Jack's death, he still did not trust Corey. As the latter passed, Red kept his gun steadily on him.

As Butch and Slip stepped aside they both holstered their weapons. At the door Corey turned and said 'You'll have to watch your steps. Winters' men are after you. I couldn't convince 'em that you weren't the men they wanted.'

'We'll watch out,' said Red gruffly. 'Lead on.'

As Corey led them down the passage he told them as much as he knew about the shooting and his conclusion that it had been a fair fight.

'I guess it had to happen sooner or later,' said Slip. 'Jack had bin carryin' a gun for Winters quite a few years.'

'They took Winters' body down the funeral parlour,' said Corey dispassionately. 'I wouldn't have such carrion in my saloon. I can't stand a man who pretends to be what he isn't.'

They came out into the bar room, went along the bar and began to ascend the stairs. Red had holstered his gun now but he still kept a wary eye on Corey. The other two were looking around them. It was too early in the morning for any real drinking. Now that all the shooting was over and the place cleaned up most of the onlookers had gone back to breakfast or bed. There were a few folks in the bar but nobody who the partners recognized. Any or all of them might be Winters' men.

They were not long to remain in doubt for a big florid-faced *hombre* suddenly rose from a table beneath the stairs and menaced them with two guns.

He looked up to them in a line on the

steps above him and rasped:

'Stand right there. We want you!'

Red was on the bottom step. He acted. His draw was a thing of wonder. His hip was wreathed in smoke as his right hand gun crashed. It was a desperate chance. But they were desperate people. The big man had taken an awful chance in holding up three such lobos single-handed. The heavy slug hit him in the shoulder and spun him round. He dropped one gun but did not go down and as he regained his balance, the other was still in his hand. He was game — the marshal had not deserved such a man — but he could not do much now he was menaced by three guns. He let his own weapon clatter to the floor, and stood there swaying a little, looking up at them with hot, fearless eyes. His hand gripped his shoulder, the blood was beginning to trickle through his fingers, his florid face began to pale. His pard at the same table placed his hands, palm downwards, on the table-top.

The big lawman said: 'You're fast, brother.'

'Yeh,' said Red. 'You better get that shoulder fixed, brother.'

On the stairs the three partners, each with a gun that menaced the occupants of the room, were an awesome trio. Jim Corey stood on the top of the stairs.

He said, clearly and slowly. 'I don't want any more shooting in my saloon so I'd be obliged if all of you people down there would give your guns to my barman.'

The plump bartender, for the second time that day, was an object of interest. He made the most of it. He brought his sawn-off shotgun up above the bar and levelled it at the half-dozen or so folks.

'Park your hardware right here aside o' me, gentlemen,' he said. 'One at a time, please.'

Menaced as they were by a whole battery of artillery the disgruntled customers were compelled to obey orders.

'If anybody tries any funny business

I'll fill 'em full o' buckshot,' said the bartender. He began to toss the assorted conglomeration of deadly weapons in a corner behind the bar, well out of everyone's reach.

Corey spoke to the wounded man. 'You'd better come on up here and let me fix that shoulder.'

Looking somewhat surprised at such humane treatment the big lawman began to mount the stairs.

A minute or so later he was having his wound dressed quite competently by King Corey who told him he had throwed-down on the wrong bozoes and he was lucky he was not dead meat. Meanwhile in an adjoining room, the three partners were gathered silently around the body of Jack Berners laid out it seemed by almost reverent hands, on a truckle bed. Berners had been shot up pretty badly but his eyes were closed and he looked kind of peaceful.

Slip said: 'I guess he always figured it would come to this. He had to get Winters but he wasn't the sort of guy who'd do it any other way but the straightest. He had to take this chance with a fast-drawin' man like that one. I'm glad he got him, too.'

'Such a darned waste though,' said Red savagely. 'One good guy for a snake like that. I could've taken him.'

'Yeh, Red, we know,' said Slip gently. 'But it wasn't *your* brother he killed.'

'No,' Red shrugged. 'Wal, I guess it couldn't be helped nohow.'

Butch had not spoken. With movements surprisingly delicate for a man of his size he drew the sheet once more over Berners' face.

'Come on, boys,' he said. 'I guess Jack's purty happy wherever he is. We still got lots to do.'

The words could have been a cynical mockery but Butch wasn't made that way. Coming from him they could not be anything but sincere. The three men filed from the room.

Corey was watching the big lawman, his arm in a sling, going down the stairs. They heard Corey say: 'Remember what I told you.'

He turned as Red said: 'You're lettin' him go?'

'Yes, he's had his fangs pulled. My barman's got his guns.' He looked down the stairs again. 'He's going outside.'

'Probably gone to fetch his pals,' said Red.

'I don't think so. I told him all about you boys.'

'Anyway, we gotta get ridin',' said Slip. 'Them two killers are still on the loose up in the hills.'

'I'll send some o' my boys up with you,' said Corey. 'Some o' them who ain't got a grudge against the big feller here,' he indicated Butch, 'boys I can trust.'

'There's no need,' said Red. 'We'd sooner tackle 'em ourselves. It's our party.'

'Yeh,' agreed Slip and Butch.

Corey shrugged. 'Just as you say. Come and have a drink with me before you go. I'd like to talk some more about

Jack Berners and sort of arrange things.'

The three partners exchanged glances. They then followed the saloon-owner. He had two rooms upstairs here, one for living and one for sleeping. He led them into the former.

'Take a seat, boys,' he said, 'while I whip up something really good.'

Butch and Red sat rather gingerly on a rich maroon velvet couch. Slip draped himself across an armchair of the same type. This room, in the midst of the squalor of Sarido and the garish decorativeness of the saloon below, was luxurious and tasteful. The partners, with the possible exception of the phlegmatic Slip, were a little awed by it. The heavy bodies of Red and Butch sank into the softness of the couch and they leaned forward warily ready to spring, as if they suspected the unoffending piece of furniture was endeavouring to entrap them. They looked around.

In the centre of the room was a

heavy mahogany table with elaborately decorated legs as thick as sizeable treetrunks. Four chairs with intricately carved backs matched this monster. The whole outfit shone like rich wine. There was a mahogany roll-top desk twice as big as the one downstairs and a bookcase to match which was chockfull of fearsome looking leather volumes. On the walls were paintings which, if the boys had known anything about such things, they would have instantly recognized as first-rate. On the polished hardwood floor was strewn a profusion of costly mats and carpets. The place looked more like the abode of a wealthy lawyer or minister than the hideout of a crooked saloon-owner and gambler.

Corey had gone into the bedroom. Through the half-open door the partners could see enough to assure them that this chamber was as luxurious as the living-room.

The saloon-owner came through carrying a tray with four glasses.

He handed them round. 'A little concoction of my own, boys,' he said. 'I hope you'll like it.'

Red, used to tossing raw whiskey down his leathery throat, took a swig. His eyes bugged from his head and he gasped for breath.

'Jumpin' gophers!' he said when his spluttering had subsided. 'Firewater!'

'I was just going to tell you to take it easy,' said Corey.

Red eyed him suspiciously. Butch and Slip each took a sip.

Slip nodded his head. 'Good,' he said. Butch merely grunted with pleasure. Corey sat down and took a sip from his own glass. Red watched them, then he tried himself.

He smacked his lips. 'Yeh, I guess I was a mite hasty,' he said in mollified tones.

Corey opened a drawer in the desk at his elbow and brought forth a box of cheroots. He handed them round. They lit up.

Then Slip spoke. When occasion

demanded he was the gent of the trio. 'We're grateful for your hospitality, Mr Corey, but we can't let it hinder us. Them two killers might be fixing to make a getaway from the hills right now.'

'They're more likely to hole-up till they think the heat's died down,' said the saloon-man.

'We can't take too big a chance on that,' said Slip. 'You said we'd talk about Jack Berners. Maybe you'd like tuh tell us how you come to be a friend o' his.'

Corey studied the glowing end of his cheroot. 'Jack and I didn't seem to have much in common did we?' he said. 'I met him first years ago when he was surveying for the railroad. They were figuring on building a line up here. I guess if they had Sarido would've been ten times this size by now. I'd've welcomed it myself. But I guess the bigwigs finally said No. Jack was . . . '
Corey suddenly paused. The others were alert too at the sound of a series of

bumps from downstairs.

Suddenly an agonized voice yelled: 'Boss!' and seemed to be cut off short as if a strong hand had closed on a windpipe. There was a crash.

The four men sprang to their feet and made for the door. Slip was outside first, with Corey close behind him. Butch and Red ensconced in the couch as they were, proved a little slower in rising. But Red's draw was as fast as ever and he looked murderous.

Slip reached the head of the stairs then drew back as shots boomed. The slugs smacked into the wall.

'It's that big feller,' he said. 'An' he's got others with him.'

Corey smiled thinly as he drew his own gun. 'I'm getting too trusting in my old age,' he said. 'I thought he believed what I told him about you boys.'

'Maybe you told him to come back an' make sure,' snarled Red. He jabbed the saloon-man in the back with the barrel of his gun.

Shocked out of his usual poise Corey turned and burst out, 'Don't be a fool, man. D'you think I'd ask him to come back here and shoot at me too. I'm here with you aren't I? And for all I know they might've killed my barman.'

Slip snapped a shot downstairs. 'They've taken cover,' he said. 'I suppose they figured in surprising us. But it ain't worked.' He turned. 'We ain't got time to fight amongst ourselves now,' he said crisply. Then to Corey — 'Is this the only way down?'

'Yes.'

'We gotta get out of here somehow,' Slip said. 'We cain't stop here all morning swopping shots with these bozos.'

'You could try the windows,' said Corey. 'The one in my room is right above the awning. It isn't a very long drop.'

'Cover the stairs,' said Slip. 'I'll go take a look.'

He vanished. A second or so later shots sounded from outside. Slip came running back. 'They've got men out there as well,' he said.

Red cursed and flung himself on to the landing. He reclined, triggering furiously. Somebody yelled. Red crawled back.

'I plugged somebody's arm,' he said disgustedly. 'they're suttinly keepin' well covered.' He grinned, still the unpredictable Red. 'Maybe they're figurin' on starving us out.'

Slip said to Corey, 'Could they get up tuh that window o' yourn from down in the street?'

'They could try,' said the saloon-owner. 'It wouldn't be hard to get up on the hitching-rack and shin up a post.'

'I'll go cover that,' said the lean ranny and he sped away.

Almost immediately his gun began to boom. Retaliatory fire made the din hideous for a moment. Then it died down.

'You all right, Slip?' yelled Butch.

'Yeh,' came the answer. 'I wuz just in time.' A pause, then: 'There ain't a soul

254

in sight out here now . . . Now listen.'

The others listened. What Slip meant to do they did not know but suddenly the racket started all over again.

When it had subsided Slip shouted: 'I never did like that hat. Right now it'd make a good sieve. There's quite an army down there. You got a rifle, friend Corey?'

'Yes, in the bedroom.'

They heard Slip moving about. They heard him settle again. Then the rifle began to crack.

'He's a wizard with one o' them things,' said Butch. 'I guess them bozoes outside dassent roll their eyes in case the whites show.'

He turned his attention suddenly to the stairs again as, fanning the hammer of his left-hand gun, Red sent a stream of hot lead sizzling down there. The law-party retaliated but their shots went wide. They seemed to be content to bide their time until the others tried to make a break.

'The floor,' said Corey suddenly. 'It's

wood and it isn't too thick. Fire through the floor.' He suited the action to words.

Down below somebody gave an agonized yell.

'Let 'em have some more,' said Red. 'C'mon Butch.'

As Corey triggered once more the two men dived for the stairs and began blasting. Behind a withering hail of two-gun fire they began to descend.

The lawmen, taking two wounded with them, had moved from under the stairs and out of the range of Corey's fire. They had taken cover behind upturned tables in the body of the saloon and, as the two pardners got halfway down the stairs they had to dive for safety from more flying lead. From behind the uncertain cover of the balustrade they retaliated.

'We gotta get back,' said Butch.

Unaware of the attackers' movements and probably thinking he was being covered by the other two, Corey suddenly appeared at the top of the stairs. Before he could bring his guns to line every lawman in the place shot at him. His somersaulting body almost knocked Red and Butch from their precarious perches.

They caught hold of him and dragged him back to the top. Red had a slight flesh-wound in his thigh. Butch was unhurt.

In the cover of the landing once more they bent over Corey. He was not a pretty sight.

'He's bin kind of careless all along,' said Butch. 'Maybe it's because he's bin so used to bein' king-pin here.'

Red muttered something under his breath and, turning, essayed a couple more shots around the corner. The veritable hail of lead that followed made a sorry mess of the wall at the top of the stairs.

2

At the window of the room overlooking the street Slip Anderson was enjoying

257

himself. With his chin cradled in the stock of the Smith & Wesson repeating rifle, his keen eyes alert, he felt like a king. The crown of a Stetson showed for a moment above the rim of a water-butt across the street. Slip squeezed the trigger. The rifle jerked and spat. The hat disappeared. The sound of a curse followed the echoes of the shot in the still air.

Slip didn't think he'd done anybody any really grievous harm as yet; the attackers were keeping too well hidden for that. They knew by now that they were up against a sharpshooter. If anybody got themselves killed Slip figured that was just too bad. Many of the men down there were lawmen who thought they were doing their duty and he didn't want to kill any of that sort if it could be helped. The mere joy of marksmanship meant more to him than any joy he might get from seeing men's lives snuffed out by his hand. But they'd better not press him too hard or he'd lay 'em in the street without hesitation . . . However, right now nobody seemed inclined to do any pressing.

But Slip was not deluded. He kept well away from the window and awaited the hail of lead which he knew they'd send at him, covering as some of them made a break.

He wondered how the other three were faring. Since that last hellish spate of shooting they were silent.

He shouted: 'Red! Butch! You all right?'

Butch replied: 'Yeh, we are. But Corey ain't.'

Slip was surprised. He shrugged. After that he did not have any more time to think about it right then. The artillery had opened up down below and slugs were whipping through the window like a swarm of furious bees.

He was in cover and he kept like that — watching the hot lead trace a pattern on the opposite wall, the top of the door and, in particular, a picture that hung right in the line of fire. The picture was of a rushing mountain torrent, tall trees, a blue haze of mountains and sky in the background. The scene was being lost forever as the painting was torn to ribbons. Rather that than my guts thought Slip without a single shudder.

He turned and looked obliquely through the window. Two men were running across the street. Slip sighted the rifle and squeezed the trigger. Both men went down, one of them kicking on his back like a skinny beetle. The other rose to his knees, fanning the hammer of his gun. Two slugs almost took Slip's nose off. He drew back swiftly. Phew!

When he looked again the sharp-shooter was dragging his pard back to cover while the battery continued to pour lead into the room. He didn't risk another pot at them. He fell flat and wriggled to the other side of the window. Just as he figured: they were crossing on that side too. Three men. They spotted him and began blasting. He drew back. Placed as he was he could not get a bead on them. He pointed the rifle in their general direction and emptied it. A slug ricocheted from the barrel and buried itself in the velvet back of the couch. The shooting stopped suddenly.

Slip wasn't aware of the fact right away. His head was still singing, his blood hot. Then he heard the sound of galloping horses. The sound was coming nearer down the street; soon they would pass beneath the window. But here they stopped.

Slip peeped round the edge of the curtain. He felt like whooping aloud at what he saw but, for a moment, his natural caution forbade it. Almost directly below his window was the mounted figure of his old sheriff, Abel Kent of Scarsville. Beside him was another man, a hard-looking customer whose face seemed familiar to Slip. And behind them was a small bevy of mounted men, many of whom the lean ranny recognized as old acquaintances.

Abel, the old buzzard! Slip figured he

ought to've known the ol' sidewinder would turn up not so far behind the Winters mob. These latter were leaving cover now and, vociferating volubly, were gathering around the old sheriff and his companion. The latter was obviously someone of importance.

Slip crossed the room and went out into the passage. 'Boys,' he said. 'Abel Kent's here with a bunch o' men. Looks like they're drawin' the others off.'

'Yeh,' said Red. 'The bunch below seemed to be goin' out to investigate. This is our chance to get away.'

'I guess we'd better make our presence known to Abel first,' said Slip.

'Yeh, I guess that would be best,' said Red. Butch grunted assent.

'Hang on here,' said Slip and he returned to the window.

He moved aside the curtain and yelled: 'Sheriff Kent. Abel Kent!'

The old man looked up. He knew that voice.

'Thet you, Slip?'

'Yeh.'

Abel turned and exchanged a few words with the hard faced man at his side. Then he yelled: 'Hold on, Slip. I'm comin' up.'

Still hidden in case one of the Winters boys took a notion to have a pot at him, Slip watched the old man dismount and cross the street. He ran back to tell the others.

They met Abel in the passage.

'You crazy young coyotes,' he greeted them. 'I never ought to've let you outa my sight. I suppose it's a case o' mistaken identity again is it?' he jeered.

The young coyotes opined it was and told their story quickly.

Finally Slip said: 'Who's that galloot you got with yuh, Abel?'

'You remember him don't yuh? That's Marshal Clem Powers. You've met him.'

'Oh, yeh, I remember now. Coupla years ago. He got Brazos Jackson didn't he? Who's he after now?'

'Jim Corey. Seems they finally built

the full case against him. Powers had orders from right back East. He's wanted for everything in the book.'

'So he might be,' said Red surprisingly. 'But he played square with us. That's what's left of him.' He indicated the still form in the corner.

'Powers will be disappointed,' said Abel. 'By the way, he ain't no friend o' Winters either. I tol' him all about you boys.'

'He needn't worry about Winters either,' said Butch, 'Jack Berners got him.'

'Jack? Where is he?'

Butch shook his head slowly. 'Jack 'ud be mighty sorry he couldn't be here tuh meet yuh.'

'Abel,' said Red, raring to go at once. 'We gotta get after them two killers up in the hills.'

'I ain't gonna try to stop yuh,' said the old sheriff. 'I know by now that it ain't no use anyway. You'd better go out the back way in case any of Winters' boys still have warlike intentions. I want

these men as badly as you do. Me an'
the boys won't be far behind yuh.'

He descended the stairs with them
into the now deserted bar room. The
fat bartender was holding his head in
a corner behind the bar. Abel shook
hands with his three erstwhile
deputies.

'I'll be seein' yuh, boys,' he said.

They left him and went out back to
their horses. A few minutes later they
were making their way up into the hills.

It was the keen-eyed Slip who
spotted the smoke.

'Up ahead,' he said. 'Come on.'

By tortuous ways they finally reached
the little cabin in the small clearing
amid the pinnacles. They advanced on
it warily. But they need not have
bothered. In more ways than one the
little place was like a grave. The fat
body of Monty was already cold but
mutely told its own story of treachery
and greed.

'I allus figured that wolf-faced runt
was the meanest one o' the three,' said

Red, and unconsciously he rubbed his head. He had plenty good reason to remember Lafe.

The three men went outside again to the small fire that had been the means of guiding them there. It was just a bundle of smouldering dry grass.

'He probably lit that to draw us here,' said Slip. 'Knowing it'd take time to burn through an' start smokin'.'

'Now he's on his own an' with all that boodle I guess there's only one place he'd make for,' said Red.

'Back to civilization,' said Butch.

'Shore thing.'

Slip was prowling. He had already picked up what looked like the beginnings of a fresh trail.

'Bring the hosses,' he said. 'I shouldn't think he'd risk movin' around here until it was light. Too treacherous. Maybe he didn't figure we'd find the hideout so soon. He cain't be very far in front.'

Lafe had more than the average share of vile traits in his make-up. Not the least of them was his inherent sadism and brutality, an almost bestial lust to kill even when there was no reason for it. This trait, coupled with his insatiable greed, finally swung the rope that it had steadily but surely knit for him.

For another fortnight he was a one-man wave of terror across the West, then Fate called a halt, figuring no doubt that it was time tardy retribution took a hand. It was no coincidence that the vessel of retribution was right there, it had been dogging Lafe's footsteps for many weary, heartbreaking miles, following the trail of blood and sorrow he left behind him — a trail little less terrible than those blazed by the James' boys, the Youngers, Billy the Kid, Sam Bass and others in their most atrocious heydey.

Just outside the little town of Hobville, Lafe's horse stumbled in a gopher-hole and lamed itself. Lafe stole a horse from a farm. The farmer's wife came out yelling. Lafe turned and shot her in the leg. She was lucky.

He found it easier to get new horses than to rest the same mount all the time. Keepers of feed stables were notorious gossips. He bivouaced in the open. He was used to that. When he wanted food he stole it. That was better than going to crowded eating places in towns where people might notice him. He was very cunning and very deadly.

Just outside Stockton he held up a store. He killed the old proprietor and took food and money. As if he was not already hauling enough of the latter. The proprietor's daughter tried to give the alarm. He did not kill her but he served her badly in other ways. Still, maybe she was lucky, too.

It would have been better for him had he killed her because finally she put a posse on his trail. He was clever. He shook them off. But he was beginning to act more like a hunted animal every day.

A doctor was driving a two-horse buggy along a lonely trail. Lafe held him up, killed him and took the best of the two horses, as well as the dead man's rifle. At a small ranch where he later called for a drink for himself and his horse somebody recognized the rifle. It was of a distinctive pattern and had its owner's initials on the stock. As soon as Lafe was challenged he drew his guns. He killed two men and a horse and escaped with a few scratches himself. But he raised a real hue-and-cry this time. His three worst enemies caught up with the tail-end of the chase.

By this time Lafe was moving into the Pecos, into the maze of hills which he knew so well, the owlhooter's paradise. But Red, Butch and Slip knew the hills very well too. They had been raised in their shadows.

Lafe did not know what a tragic mistake he had made when he holed-up in that certain brush-covered dip in the hills and sat back complacently. He figured he'd rest up a mite. Then in a few days when things were quieter he'd push on. For New Mexico, Arizona, California, luxury and the easy life! And plenty of pickings on the way to boot!

It was a horse's cry that warned him just after dawn that morning. In the shadows Butch Keaters cursed softly and grabbed the nose of his precious brown stallion with unusual violence.

Red said: 'If I hear another squeal out o' that critter I'll stun him.'

The three men waited silently, looking across the gentle grassy clearing before them to the small glade where lay their quarry.

Lafe was squatting on his haunches waiting and listening too. He could've sworn he had heard a horse whinny. Maybe it was his own. Although it had sounded a distance away. He had been half-asleep, maybe he had imagined it. His own horse seemed quite undisturbed, cropping grass there on the edge of the clearing. It was a silent, peaceful morning. No breeze, no sound.

Lafe shrugged his shoulders, grinned his snaggle-toothed grin and walked across to his horse.

'Here he is,' hissed Slip.

Red grasped his arm. 'He's mine,' he said. 'I owe him more than either of you.'

Slip looked at Butch. Butch shrugged. The only man he'd known who was faster than Red didn't exist any more. He had fallen from his horse and broken his neck.

'All right,' whispered Slip.

Red gave his gunbelt a little hitch with both hands then strode forth into the clearing.

Lafe saw him immediately and turned away from his horse. It was too late however to turn back now. He stood and waited. He was surprised to see there was only one man. The cocky redhead!

He spread his feet and crouched a

little. He threw his weight on the balls of his feet. His hands were lax and open but his arms were slightly bent. He watched the redhead come nearer.

The latter walked with long catlike strides. He looked almost sinister in the early morning light, his feet almost hidden in a soft blue ground mist. His face was expressionless. His eyes didn't seem to be looking at anything in particular. They were hard and glass-like. He kept coming.

Lafe's lips curled in a wolfish travesty of a smile, showing the ends of his yellow fangs. He waited till the redhead got a little bit nearer, till he took another step and seemed a mite off-balance. Then he went for his guns.

Red saw the first shudder of move-ment and, with one knee bent, the other out straight behind him, moved with icy smoothness, too.

Even as his thumbs pressed the hammers something hot and heavy seemed to push him violently and the morning light became a haze. He continued firing mechanically through the haze and just before it turned to total darkness he knew he had got his man.

When he came to, the hazy but quite familiar faces of his two partners seemed to be floating in nothingness above him.

He opened his mouth and croaked. 'God, the little runt was fast. I never seen anybody so fast. It seems he manages to clout me every time.'

'You went one better than him this time, pardner,' were the last words he heard before blackness enveloped him once more.

★ ★ ★

When Red came round again he found himself in a room with pretty flowers all over the walls. Further investigation proved to him that he was tucked between white sheets in a deliriously soft bed. His body felt queer. As if it didn't quite belong to him any more.

He discovered he was bound tightly round and round with bandage.

He suddenly remembered that Abel Kent had a bedroom like this one. But of course this could not be it. Maybe they had bedrooms like this in Heaven!

The door opposite him slowly opened and an angel appeared. She was dressed all in white. Her hair was more golden than the shimmering summer range, her eyes were bluer than the Texas skies. And she had the sweetest smile Red had ever seen. He hadn't thought that even angels could be as beautiful as that.

Quite naturally he suddenly remembered the angel's name.

'Ann,' he said.

'Hallo, Red,' she replied. Her voice was like the merry tinkle of a brook in spring.

She came closer and, bending over him, kissed him gently on the forehead.

Red suddenly discovered he could move his arms. He brought them forth and put them around her.

'Gosh,' he said and drew her closer to him.